REA

P9-EDX-687

3 1833 03610 2538

"Doesn't a little boy's request mean anything to you?"

Rafe's brows snapped together in a dark, threatening way. "The last thing I want to be is a substitute father for this boy."

"How about just being his friend?"

"I'm not the hero he believes I am," he stated in a dangerously soft voice, "and this ranch isn't equipped for kids."

Lauren stood and approached him, feeling reckless enough to challenge him. She stopped close enough to draw in the warm male scent of him, to feel the heat of his body. Close enough to see the awareness flare to life in his pewter eyes.

"One boy, Mr. Dalton, not a whole slew of them. Chad is so enamored of you he'll take what few crumbs of time you have to offer—"

"No." This time his tone lacked its original harshness. "And I apologize for not responding to your letters, because it would have saved you a wasted trip."

Ch

Br

What kind of man makes the perfect husband?

A man with a big heart and strong arms—someone tough
but tender, powerful yet passionate...

And where can such a man be found?

In our brand-new miniseries:

Marriages made on the ranch...

Look out for these Western weddings throughout 2000
in Harlequin Romance®.

Substitute
Father
Janelle Denison

TORONTO • NEW YORK • LONDON
AMSTERDAM • PARIS • SYDNEY • HAMBURG
STOCKHOLM • ATHENS • TOKYO • MILAN • MADRID
PRAGUE • WARSAW • BUDAPEST • AUCKLAND

If you purchased this book without a cover you should be aware
that this book is stolen property. It was reported as "unsold and
destroyed" to the publisher, and neither the author nor the
publisher has received any payment for this "stripped book."

To Grandma Margie, Grandma Madeline and Grandpa Rial;
thank you for adding extra love and warmth to my life.
You all are very special to me.

And as always, to Don, for being the love of my life, and
for being a constant reminder of why I write about
romance and happily-ever-afters.

ISBN 0-373-03597-7

SUBSTITUTE FATHER

First North American Publication 2000.

Copyright © 1999 by Janelle R. Denison.

All rights reserved. Except for use in any review, the reproduction or
utilization of this work in whole or in part in any form by any electronic,
mechanical or other means, now known or hereafter invented, including
xerography, photocopying and recording, or in any information storage
or retrieval system, is forbidden without the written permission of the
publisher, Harlequin Enterprises Limited, 225 Duncan Mill Road,
Don Mills, Ontario, Canada M3B 3K9.

All characters in this book have no existence outside the imagination of
the author and have no relation whatsoever to anyone bearing the same
name or names. They are not even distantly inspired by any individual
known or unknown to the author, and all incidents are pure invention.

This edition published by arrangement with Harlequin Books S.A.

® and TM are trademarks of the publisher. Trademarks indicated with
® are registered in the United States Patent and Trademark Office, the
Canadian Trade Marks Office and in other countries.

Visit us at www.romance.net

Printed in U.S.A.

CHAPTER ONE

IT HAD been one of the longest days of Lauren Richmond's life. A five-hour flight out of LAX to Cody, Wyoming, had turned into a ten-hour nightmare of airline delays and layovers, not to mention the added two-hour drive in a rental car to Cedar Creek, the small town south of Cody where Rafe Dalton lived. It was after seven in the evening, the day nearly gone, though the warm June sun still hung against the endless expanse of blue sky.

Lauren was exhausted and hungry, and the more she thought about Rafe Dalton's rudeness, which had forced her to make this impromptu trip from Los Angeles, the more agitated she became. This formal visit could have been avoided by a simple return phone call in response to any of the three registered letters she'd sent him. A signed receipt was proof that he'd received her correspondences, yet he hadn't had the courtesy to acknowledge any of them.

Lauren tightened her grip on the steering wheel of her rented sedan and blew out a frustrated stream of breath that ruffled the wispy bangs brushing across her forehead. Rafe Dalton might be a hotshot, three-time Professional Rodeo Cowboy's Association Bull Riding Champion, but in her estimation he was an arrogant, self-centered boar!

As much as she dreaded meeting the man, a confrontation was inevitable. A nine-year-old boy was counting on her to make his fondest wish come true, and she'd yet to disappoint any of her young foster clients. No matter how inconsiderate the man, she refused to allow Rafe Dalton to be her first failure.

She passed numerous houses and ranches, their addresses indicating she was headed in the right direction. Before long she came upon a crude dirt road that disappeared over a small crest and didn't invite exploration. Slowing her vehicle, she scanned the area and found the verification she needed. Posted at the entrance was a sturdy metal mailbox imprinted with the address she was looking for, along with the name R. Dalton. Below that was a bright red sign stating Private Road. No Trespassing.

Ignoring the blatant warning, she turned her car onto the bumpy dirt drive. After everything she'd gone through to get here, she wasn't about to be intimidated by a road that seemingly vanished over a knoll or a sign warning away strangers. She refused to leave Wyoming until she spoke face-to-face to the bull-riding champion and convinced him to oblige her client. Certainly once he understood her purpose he'd be more accommodating.

What she encountered when her vehicle crested the small hill caused a frown to form on her brow. She'd heard Rafe Dalton was fairly wealthy from his PRCA winnings. She'd expected something far grander than what met her eyes. About half a mile down the road, standing in a sheltering copse of cottonwoods, was a simple one-story timber structure with a small porch. There was nothing elaborate or pretentious about the house, nothing to indicate the man who resided there lived in the lap of luxury. In fact, as she drove closer, she decided the place lacked color and panache. And warmth.

Beyond the modest house and small, neat yard, a large white barn and other utility buildings fanned out in a half circle, connected to each other by a network of corrals and pens. To her left, horses grazed lazily in a huge, sprawling pasture.

She pulled her car next to a shiny red truck parked on a paved area in front of the house and cut the engine. She gathered her purse and briefcase, then stepped out of the vehicle and rolled her stiff shoulders as she glanced around, waiting for that friendly country hospitality everyone told her she'd encounter from the people who lived in the mid-west. No one came to greet her. In fact, except for the soft neighing of horses and the twittering of a few birds, everything was quiet.

In a last-ditch effort to look presentable and professional after her long, tiring day, Lauren ran her fingers through the blunt cut of her shoulder-length hair and smoothed a hand down her light-blue linen skirt. She was certain she looked as wilted as she felt, but she knew there was little she could do about her unfashionable state. She headed determinedly toward Rafe Dalton's house.

Her heels clicked on the stairs and echoed off the wooden porch. The front door stood open, the entryway secured by a screen door inlaid with solid oak. Inside, the house was silent.

Lauren knocked on the wooden slat on the screen door and anxiously waited for a response. She prided herself on being confident when it came to business, yet she couldn't stop the sudden attack of nerves that swarmed in her belly. She had no idea what to expect from this man she'd traveled thousands of miles to visit on a little boy's behalf. She only knew she'd do everything in her power to return to California with good news for her young, hopeful foster client, Chad Evans.

When she received no reply, she knocked again, louder and harder this time, a resounding rap no one in the house could dismiss. A few seconds later she heard heavy footsteps heading toward the foyer.

"I'm comin', Kristin," a gruff male voice announced, the tone brusque. "And when did you develop manners to knock instead of barging in like you normally do—"

His words abruptly died when he saw that the person standing on his porch wasn't the woman he'd been expecting. As far as Lauren knew from the reports she'd been given on Rafe Dalton, he was unmarried, so she assumed Kristin was a lady friend.

The man glaring at her through the screen door was without a doubt Rafe Dalton, bull-riding champion extraordinaire. And it looked as though she'd caught him fresh out of the shower. He wore a pair of faded jeans that rode low on his hips, and nothing else.

Her heart thumped in her chest and her mouth went dry, making speech impossible. His midnight black hair was damp and tousled around his head, and droplets of water still clung to the light furring of hair on his wide and well-defined chest. His shoulders were broad, his arms roped with muscle and sinew. A flat belly tapered into narrow hips, which gave way to hard thighs and long, strong legs.

Lord, the man was gorgeous, if you didn't count the tight clenching of his firm, chiseled jaw, which gave him a dark and dangerous edge she hadn't detected in any of the pictures Chad had eagerly shared with her. The multitude of candid photographs from Chad's scrapbook had shown a man in his prime, a sexy, swaggering cowboy with a cocky sparkle in his light gray eyes and a friendly, flirtatious smile that no doubt had many rodeo bunnies vying for his attention.

Retirement hadn't been kind to him. Though the man in front of her was in his prime physically, there was a darkness in his narrowed gaze as intense and chilling as a fierce, brooding storm. There was no warmth in his eyes, no reckless charm in his expression, just a bleak emptiness that didn't invite a person to breach the dark barriers he'd erected.

He didn't bother to open the screen door, the gesture a sign that she wasn't welcome. His gaze flickered down the length of her, taking in her cream silk blouse, linen skirt and strappy summer heels with unnerving insolence.

"You lost or something, lady?" he asked, the lines above his brows deepening in a fierce frown. "You're about two hours away from where you belong."

His harsh greeting startled her. "Excuse me?"

He propped his hands on his hips, agitation radiating from him. "Dressed like you are, I'm guessing you're not from around here."

She did suppose her attire was more sophisticated than this rural part of Wyoming warranted. "No, I'm not—"

"Didn't think so." He cut her off before she could finish. "Cody is north of here. Hop back on the interstate, and it's a straight shot from there." He turned to leave, clearly dismissing her, then abruptly stopped and glanced back. "And the next time you see a Private Road, No Trespassing sign posted, it means keep out, unless you're issued a personal invitation.''

Indignation bristled up Lauren's spine. The man wasn't only rude, but insulting, to boot! Before he could turn away again and she lost the opportunity to state her business, she said, ''I'm not looking for the nearest city. I just drove from Cody, after spending eight hours trying to get to Wyoming from Los Angeles.'' Her tone was curt and fringed with the beginnings of anger. ''I'm here to talk to *you*, Mr. Dalton.'' The fact that she knew who he was and had made a special trip to see him snagged his attention. He gave her another once-over that was slow, thorough and made her skin tingle in an unsettling way.

''And you are?'' he asked in a low, rumbling drawl, though his soft tone didn't make up for his grim expression.

''Lauren Richmond.'' Her chin lifted in a show of defiance and tenacity, and her fingers tightened around the handle of her leather briefcase. ''And if the name sounds familiar, it's because I'm the woman who sent you *three* certified letters, none of which you had the courtesy of replying to.''

Her speech ended on a peak of displeasure. He remained aloof and uninfluenced, his gaze cool and detached. It was as though the man just didn't care…about anything.

He shifted on his bare feet, transferring his weight to his left leg. ''Did it ever occur to you that I'm not interested in whatever it is you're selling?''

Resentment blossomed within Lauren. How could anyone *not* be interested in her foundation's purpose? She opened her mouth to issue a scathing reply to such an insensitive, cold remark, then snapped it shut as realization dawned. "Did you even read those letters I sent?"

"Nope."

He didn't have the courtesy to show a little guilt over his negligence! "May I ask why not?"

"Like I said, I'm not interested in whatever it is you're selling." His tone held a hint of censure along with a dose of impatience. "Looks like you wasted a trip, Miz Richmond."

Lauren released a breath, but the tension gathering within her didn't ease. She resented the screen door between them—it made her feel like the salesperson he believed she was—but he didn't seem inclined to invite her inside.

After the incredibly long day she'd endured, her tolerance had reached its limit. "Mr. Dalton," she began, deliberately using a placating tone of voice, as if she were dealing with a small child with a cantankerous disposition. "I'm not here to *sell* you anything. I'm here on behalf of a client. And I would have called first, but your number isn't listed."

"I don't have a phone," he said abruptly, his gaze narrowing with shrewd intent. "You a lawyer?"

If the man wasn't such a grouch, she would have smiled. Unfortunately, she didn't think he'd appreciate her humor. "No, I'm a foster care assistant, and I also represent Bright Beginnings."

Confusion touched his expression, enough to tell her he honestly hadn't given her letters, or the return address, a second glance. "What, exactly, is Bright Beginnings?"

"It's a special foundation dedicated to offering foster children the opportunity to make a special request and make their future seem brighter." She couldn't help the pride in her voice. Though she worked for Blair Foster Care Services, Bright Beginnings was her personal baby, a labor of love she'd established from the substantial trust fund her grandmother had endowed to her.

He appeared unmoved. "And what does that have to do with me?"

Lauren realized this was her one chance to sway Rafe and possibly soften his surly temperament. What man wouldn't like to be idolized in the eyes of a young boy? "A client of mine made a Bright Beginnings request, and that was to meet Rafe Dalton, three-time PRCA Bull Riding Champion." This time she did smile, remembering Chad's excitement over the prospect of meeting the man he held in such high esteem. It was the first time since Chad's parents' death that she'd seen him so happy. The image of Chad's grinning face and the hope sparkling in his eyes spurred her onward. "You're his hero, and he looks up to you."

His body went rigid, and he clenched his fists at his sides. "I'm *nobody's* hero, lady, got that?" Fury blazed in his eyes.

Startled by the pure venom in his tone, she took a step back, nearly stumbling in her haste. It was like she'd lit a fuse. A very volatile one. The thunderous emotions brewing in his eyes sent a series of shivers racing down her spine, especially since all that ferocity was directed at her.

Grasping for levity to dispel the intensity of the moment, Lauren swallowed hard and found her voice. "Really, Mr. Dalton, it was meant as a compliment, not the insult you make it out to be."

A muscle in his jaw ticked. "A hero is the last thing I deserve to be called. Got that?" He bit the words out, his rough tone demanding an answer.

A few more worthy names leaped to mind, but she wasn't willing to provoke him any further by offering them. "Loud and clear," she managed to say.

Rafe Dalton certainly wasn't *her* version of a hero, she thought, but kept the derogatory remark to herself. Everyone looked up to certain people for their own reasons, and though she was seriously questioning Chad's choice of idol, she couldn't help wondering about that carefree, grinning cowboy within the pages of Chad's scrapbook. What had happened to make him so bitter?

He straightened and scrubbed a hand over his face, swearing softly beneath his breath as his anger faded. She watched the transformation, the guilt and pain reflected in his eyes in the aftermath of the fury. For a handful of seconds, he gave her the impression of a wounded animal, then the fleeting glimpse was gone.

She wasn't ready to give up, not after seeing that the man possessed more vulnerabilities than he wanted the outside world to know about. It was a weakness she used to her advantage.

"Mr. Dalton," she said softly, imploringly. "I've traveled all the way from California to talk to you. I'm tired, hungry, and my feet are killing me, so I apologize if I might have snapped at you." She heaped the blame on herself, but he wasn't impressed by her attempt to make amends for their quarrel—which *he'd* instigated. She forged on. "I'm also extremely stubborn and persistent when it comes to a client's request. Won't you let me come in for a few

minutes so we can discuss this situation more...
rationally?''

He looked at her as if she were out of her mind
for wanting to be near him after what had just transpired. ''I don't believe there's anything to discuss.''
His voice was flat, devoid of any emotion.

''Give me thirty minutes of your time. That's all
I ask.''

He eyed her beneath hooded lashes, wary and reluctant.

She put on her most persuasive expression.
''Please,'' she whispered beseechingly. ''Just thirty
minutes to explain a little more about Bright
Beginnings.'' *And to convince you that your help will
make all the difference in the world to a lonely, dis-
illusioned boy.*

His lips thinned, and he shook his head in self-
disgust. ''I'll give you fifteen,'' he said gruffly, and
pushed open the screen door for her to enter.

His generosity was overwhelming, she thought
with dry sarcasm as she stepped in before he changed
his mind. If she didn't manage to soften him up, there
was no way she'd introduce Chad to him and dash
the boy's sterling image of Rafe Dalton.

She followed Rafe toward an adjoining room,
which gave her a few seconds to appreciate his
strong, broad back, the slight swagger of his hips,
and well-toned buttocks nicely displayed in soft
denim. She'd never gone for the rugged type, but he
was certainly appealing—if you overlooked that per-
petual scowl on his handsome face, which wasn't
hard to do when a woman had such a physically attractive body to admire.

It was then she noticed a barely perceptible hitch

in his walk and remembered reading in Chad's scrapbook about the injury that had ended Rafe's career as a champion bull rider. He'd been gored in the right thigh by an out-of-control bull while attempting to rescue a young rider who'd been knocked unconscious after being thrown by the beast. Judging by the way Rafe favored his right leg, she guessed the affliction still nagged him—along with the honor of being hailed a hero, a title he'd earned that fateful day. One he clearly scorned.

They entered a room furnished with a brown leather wraparound couch and a matching easy chair complemented with oak end tables and a wall-length entertainment unit that held a large-screen TV. She saw no evidence of the PRCA champion he'd been. No trophies. No plaques. No pictures. Nothing to indicate he was anything more than a simple, down-home cowboy—albeit a grouchy one.

He stopped and propped his shoulder against the door frame, his stance indolent, his expression bored. She paused beside him, waiting for an invitation to venture farther into his domain.

He wasn't a gracious host. He didn't offer her a seat, or a cool drink, which she would have welcomed. A secret smile touched Lauren's lips. Her prim and proper mother would be shocked at such atrocious manners, not to mention appalled by the fact that he was entertaining a guest without a shirt. *Uncivilized* is what Maureen Richmond would call a man like Rafe.

A long, insufferable sigh escaped him. He looked as though he was barely tolerating her, so she claimed the leather chair nearest him and got down to business. She had a lot to accomplish in fifteen minutes, her main goal to wring a little compassion from the hard-hearted hero.

"Like I mentioned before, I'm a foster care assistant. I work for Blair Foster Care Services in Pasadena, California, but I also represent Bright Beginnings, which is a foundation I personally established. It caters to helping foster children adjust to their new lives. Every once in a while I come across a young client whose extenuating circumstances warrant an extra-special request."

She pulled a manila folder from her briefcase, set it on the oak coffee table in front of her and opened it. Amongst typed reports and a Bright Beginnings application was a candid photograph of her young client. The picture of Chad depicted a smiling, healthy nine-year-old boy, but there was an acute sadness in his brown eyes, a sense of loss that reached out and grabbed at Lauren's heart. She pushed the image across the coffee table toward the man standing a few feet away, hoping the snapshot had the same effect on Rafe.

His gaze flickered briefly over the picture, then returned to Lauren, his features remaining as hard as granite.

"This is Chad Evans," she explained, unwilling to admit defeat so soon. "When he was six his father took him to the Grubstake Days PRCA Rodeo in Yucca Valley, California. You won the bull-riding event that day, and when he approached you afterward you signed his program for him."

"Do you expect me to remember one kid out of a thousand?" he asked, his tone defensive.

"I'm not asking you to remember Chad. I'm telling you this story because I want you to realize how special you made that day for him. You completely captivated him. After that rodeo he managed to follow your progress through the internet and trade publications." She smiled, absently touching the picture of the young boy. "Chad has quite an impressive scrapbook that spans the last two years of your career."

He tucked his hands beneath his arms, and the muscles across his bare chest flexed with the movement. "As short-lived as it was." Bitterness vibrated in his voice.

She offered a kind smile. "It ended on quite a crescendo."

Darkness brewed in his gaze, and she headed off volatile emotions before they sparked. "Six months ago, Chad lost both his parents in a tragic car accident. He was an only child, and he has no relatives, so he's been in foster care since their death. He's listed with an adoption program, but most couples don't want a child as old as he is. Chances are, he'll be shuffled through the system until he's eighteen, then he'll be on his own, with no family to speak of."

She glanced up in time to catch a shadow of compassion cross his expression, as if he understood a little of what the boy might be going through. Optimism bolstered her. "Chad admires you. As a person, a champion bull rider, and for risking your life to save that kid's when that bull threw him."

He stiffened, his jaw tightening. Before he could issue a heated response, she hastily wrapped up her speech. "After everything Chad has been through, I wanted to grant him a special request, something that will make his future seem a little brighter. All he

wants is to meet you and spend a few days on a real
ranch—''

"No." His tone was harsh.

"He's a wonderful boy—"

"No." Harsher still.

"Doesn't a little boy's request mean anything to
you?" she argued, not above using guilt to coerce
him.

His brows snapped together in a dark, threatening
glare. "The last thing I want to be is a substitute
father for this boy."

"How about just being his friend?"

"I'm not the hero he believes I am," he stated in
a dangerously soft voice. "And this ranch isn't
equipped for kids."

Refusing to let him think he could intimidate her
with his belligerence, she stood and approached him,
feeling reckless enough to challenge him. She
stopped so close she had to tip her head back to look
into his face. Close enough to draw in the warm male
scent of him, to feel the heat of his body. Close
enough to see the awareness flare to life in his pewter
eyes.

She was too close. He radiated unadulterated male
magnetism, raw and untamed. Her pulse quickened,
and a distinct tingle shot through her. She struggled
to get herself, and the situation, back in her control.

"One boy, Mr. Dalton, not a whole slew of them,"
she said in a calm, even voice. "Chad is so enamored
of you he'd take what few crumbs of time you had
to offer and be thrilled with just watching you."

He eased his breath out between gritted teeth, the
gesture rife with frustration. "What you do is very
noble, Miz Richmond, but Chad is better off remem-

bering the glory days rather than spending time with some washed-up bull rider.''

She shook her head. "He doesn't think of you as being washed up—''

"Exactly," he stated succinctly. "He thinks of me as the glamorous bull-riding champion I was a year ago, a cocky cowboy who believed he had the world by the tail...." He let the words trail off for her to absorb, then continued just as ruthlessly. "Well, guess what? I *am* washed up. I'm not a celebrity any longer. I'm a simple cowboy who breeds and raises Quarter Horses and prefers to be left alone. There's no glamour here, no glory and certainly no hero.''

So much hostility surrounded him, a bitterness she assumed was a result of the loss of his career. But beneath all that anger, there had to be some kindness in him, some glimpse of the friendly, warm-natured man Chad had spoken about so enthusiastically.

She tried one more time to reach him, to tell him how important this simple request was to one little boy. "Mr. Dalton—''

"Your fifteen minutes are up," he said abruptly, shoving off the doorjamb to move away.

Without thinking of the implications, she reached out and grabbed his arm before he could escape. His flesh was hard and hot beneath her hand, his strength evident in the flexing of muscle against the tips of her fingers.

He stopped and turned to her, his eyes catching fire as they clashed with hers—not with anger this time, but a more primitive emotion that touched her on a purely feminine level. That very direct, male look sent a warm shiver through her that curled low in her belly. The sensation was as shocking as it was intimate, especially since he was a stranger. He appeared just as perplexed by the sensual undercurrents shimmering between them.

Not willing to analyze something so bewildering as her attraction to such a complex man, she let go of his arm and kept her mind firmly on business. "Won't you please take a few days to reconsider your decision?"

"No." His tone lacked its original harshness. "And I apologize for not responding to your letters, because it would have saved you a wasted trip."

Just when she thought the man had no redeeming qualities, he had to reveal a more gracious side. The contrast from bad guy to nice guy intrigued her. "I would have made the trip anyway. Like I said, I'm persistent and stubborn, so don't be surprised if you hear from me again."

"Don't waste your time on me." The scowl on his face didn't quite reach his eyes. "I'm not worth pursuing."

She was beginning to seriously doubt that, but issued no verbal argument. Yes, the man seemed surrounded by some kind of personal torment and snarled when someone got too close, but Lauren suspected it was his way of dealing with whatever private demons were provoking him. She'd seen the same kind of reaction in angry young children. Adults were no different in dealing with their pain.

He looked tired and weary. Drained, even. Emotionally and physically. She decided to leave well enough alone, and hope over the next few days he'd read the letters she'd sent him. If he learned more about Bright Beginnings and how he could make a tremendous difference in the life of a young boy, maybe he'd change his mind.

She moved to where she'd been sitting, gathered the picture and information about Chad and slipped the papers into his file. Once everything was tucked into her briefcase, she faced Rafe. "I'd planned on spending the night in a hotel in Cody, but I'm too exhausted to make the two-hour drive. Is there a place nearby that I can stay?"

"The Lazy Daze motel is back about five miles, right at the edge of town next to Fran's Diner." He hesitated, then added, "It's not a very luxurious motel."

She smiled, ignoring the way he stereotyped her. "I'm not looking for something to rival the Ritz, Mr. Dalton, just a bed to sleep in for the night. I'm sure the Lazy Daze will be fine."

They walked to the foyer quietly, and he opened the screen door for her to pass through. She stepped outside, then stopped and turned to face him again.

"Please think about my client's request, Mr. Dalton, and if you change your mind, you can reach me at the motel until tomorrow morning. My flight to Los Angeles leaves at three, so I'll be gone by noon." Retrieving a business card from a side pocket in her briefcase, she handed it to him. "And here's my card, just in case you need to contact me."

He took the card but didn't give it a glance. "I suggest you head back to the city, where you belong, and find yourself another hero for your client."

"I wish it were that simple." She smiled regretfully. "Unfortunately for all of us, you're the only one Chad wants."

CHAPTER TWO

RAFE stood on the porch, shoulder braced against a wooden column. Hitching his thumbs into the front pockets of his jeans, he watched Lauren Richmond make her way to her rental car as the evening sun slowly descended toward the horizon.

Despite her unwelcome intrusion into his life, he couldn't help but admire her. The woman was passionate about what she believed in and confident about accomplishing her goal regardless of the obstacles. She came across as professional and polished, and possessed an elegance he suspected was inbred. It showed in the educated way she spoke, the keen intelligence in her pretty blue eyes, the cosmopolitan way she looked and especially the way she walked. Yeah, especially that, he thought appreciatively as he took in the natural, subtle sway of her hips and those long, sleek legs as she strolled toward her car.

A rumble of interest gripped him, the same heat and desire that had taken hold when she'd laid her hand on his. The instantaneous attraction that leaped between them had been startling and damn exciting—enough to throw him completely off-kilter. He'd been too long without the comforts of a woman, too long without someone to ease the loneliness that came with voluntary confinement.

She was the last kind of woman he should want, yet the first woman who'd affected him on an emotional and physical level since his rodeo days. City sophistication and rough-hewn country didn't mix, as he well knew. And then there were the other flaws in his character that would no doubt shock her well-bred sensibilities.

She believed he was a hero. That was the biggest reason of all to avoid her and the young boy who had such fanciful notions.

Rafe focused on the present as Lauren slipped gracefully into her rental car, blond hair swaying silkily along her shoulders, then started the engine. She looked his way, a small, friendly smile curving her mouth. She gave him a polite wave goodbye, and he squelched the automatic urge to lift his hand in response. As brash and rude as he'd been inside the house, there was no point in being courteous now and offering her any false encouragement that he might change his mind about the boy and his request.

She turned her car around and headed for the dirt drive as a blue truck crested the hill and ambled toward his house. The two vehicles passed slowly, the women in each turning her head to glance curiously at the other.

His sister had impeccable timing.

Rafe released a harsh breath between his teeth. *Great.* Just what he needed after his draining visit with Lauren Richmond—an interrogation from his inquisitive sister on who Lauren was and what she was doing at his ranch. After having his emotions rubbed raw by Miz Richmond's visit, he wasn't in the mood to deal with his sister's brand of cross-examination.

It was inevitable, he knew. Kristin cut him no slack, especially since the incident with the bull that had forced him to come home and reevaluate his life. She verbally poked and prodded him whenever the opportunity presented itself, which, unfortunately, was often, since she and her husband, James, lived on the Dalton family ranch that adjoined his property.

His sister parked the pickup next to his, slid out of the cab with a white casserole dish in hand, then headed toward the porch. Climbing the stairs, she gave him a once-over that was both chastising and mischievous. "Have you become so uncivilized that you can't throw on a shirt while entertaining a guest?" A slow grin lifted her lips, right along with a perfectly arched brow. "Or was that woman more than a guest?"

The insinuation in his sister's voice was unmistakable. He blinked lazily, maintaining a bland expression. "Does mind your own business mean anything to you?"

She was unoffended by his brush-off, and humor filled her eyes. "As much as I don't condone casual flings, it sure is nice to know that you're still human enough to enjoy a woman's company."

"It's not what you're thinking." He found having his sex life scrutinized by his sister decidedly disconcerting. Especially since he didn't have a sex life to speak of. "*She's* not what you're thinking."

"Well, then?" she prompted impatiently. "Who is she, and what does she want with you?"

In an attempt to avoid her barrage of questions and distract her, he took the casserole dish from her hands. The sight of pork chops and the mouthwatering stuffing his sister made had his stomach growling. "I wish you'd quit making extra food so you can bring me your leftovers.'' It was a lie, but a good one to divert her attention. ''I'm perfectly fine with my frozen dinners.''

She scoffed at that and smacked him lightly in the stomach. ''The least you could do for yourself with all that money you hoard is hire yourself a cook.''

''Now why would I waste my money hiring a cook when you do it for me?'' he asked in a deep, lazy drawl.

''Stop trying to change the subject, Rafe.'' Green eyes narrowed shrewdly, and she shook a finger at him. ''I find a woman out here after you've isolated yourself from the entire town for the past year, the single, available women included, and you act as though it's no big deal.''

Rafe's mouth thinned in growing annoyance. ''Trust me, I didn't invite her.''

''Ah, that makes this even more interesting,'' she said, then added on a mocking note, ''How dare she ignore that threatening sign you posted out front. I'm amazed she survived that dark scowl of yours, and your black mood.''

He summoned an ominous glower just for her, then turned on his heel and headed into the house, letting the screen door slam shut behind him. She followed, dogging his steps into the kitchen.

''So, what could a classy woman like her want with someone as moody and unsociable as you?'' she asked, picking up where she left off.

He set the casserole dish on the counter, feeling the sting of her deliberate words. Knowing there was no point in avoiding the inevitable discussion, he told her the truth about Lauren and Chad's request, and how the nine-year-old boy had followed the last two years of his career, right up until the end.

Kristin took a seat at the small oak table in the kitchen, her soft smile holding a bit of pride. "You must have made quite an impression on him."

"So it seems." He rolled his shoulders, wishing he could roll off the unwanted burden of Lauren's request as easily. "But I'm certain it won't last once she tells him I'm not available."

"You refused?" Kristin asked incredulously.

Guilt clouded Rafe's conscience, and he immediately pushed the offending emotion aside, telling himself he was saving the kid a wealth of disillusionment by declining his request.

"Quit looking at me like I'm some kind of monster," he said brusquely, feeling defensive. "There are plenty of bull-riding champions out there still traveling the circuit that would be more than willing to meet Chad and spend time with him."

She stood and moved toward him. "His wish is to meet *you*, you hard-headed oaf!" She lowered her voice until it was as soft and imploring as her moss-green eyes. "Don't you see, Rafe? This kid has placed a lot of hope in you."

"He thinks I'm a goddamn hero!" Pacing to the screen door, he braced his hand on the frame above his head and stared out to the green pasture where three Quarter Horses grazed. When the tumultuous emotions in him calmed, he said in a low voice, "I didn't ask for this. I don't want this."

"This isn't about *you*, Rafe," she replied with steadfast determination. "It's about a little boy who has lost so much and wants something that will give him a little faith in life. You obviously do that for him. And maybe, if you just gave a little of yourself, you can find the man you used to be and make peace with the man you've become.''

He clawed his hand through his thick hair and rubbed at the stiff muscles at the nape of his neck. Turning, he met his sister's gaze. ''I don't think it's possible to go back to who I was.''

''You're wrong, Rafe. You lost so much a year ago, but that kind, caring man is still there. I know he is. Deep inside, beneath all the anger and pain, is the brother that used to make me smile. And do you have any idea how long it's been since I've heard you laugh?''

Forever, it seemed. He dropped his head, sensing defeat.

''Maybe you need this kid as much as he needs you,'' Kristen said, her caring voice reaching deep inside him. ''If you can't do this for yourself, then do it for me, Rafe.''

He lifted his head, knowing he'd never be able to refuse his sister anything. She knew it, too. ''You play dirty,'' he murmured.

She lifted her shoulders in an unapologetic shrug. ''Whatever it takes to make you see reason.''

Rafe thought of a young boy with stars in his eyes. A young boy who placed Rafe on a pedestal and thought he could do no wrong. A young boy who believed he was a hero.

He shuddered. ''What do I know about kids?'' he asked gruffly. His father had hardly been a good example of parenthood.

''Probably more than you realize,'' she offered, not caving to his pitiful excuse. ''Kids are amazingly adept and have a tendency to show you what they need, and you'll instinctively know." When he gave her a look of disbelief, she smiled. "Trust me on this one, Rafe. During the school year I'm surrounded by a dozen different seven-year-old personalities, and I know what each student wants or needs before they even express it."

Doubts curled through him. "I don't know, Kristin..."

"Give the boy a week of your time, and you may change the direction of his life forever." Solemnly, she added, "Reject him, and you risk damaging his young self-esteem, especially at this stage in his life after losing both of his parents."

Finding nothing in Kristin's statement he could argue with, Rafe looked away.

"Remember how we felt after Mom died?" she asked softly.

How could he ever forget? They'd both felt so lost and confused. Except they'd had each other, and together they'd shared their grief and struggled to deal with the devastating pain of losing a sweet, loving woman, the opposite of their insensitive, apathetic father.

Chad Evans had no one to share his burdens with.

He glanced at his sister, seeing the hope in her eyes, feeling the emptiness in his chest, and knew in that single moment what he would do.

He drew a slow, steady breath and eased it out just as carefully, praying he didn't come to regret his decision. "Fine, I'll do it."

Rafe paused anxiously on the other side of Lauren's motel room door, feeling like a teenager about to pick up a date for the first time. The notion was ridiculous, considering how many women he'd been with over the years, but the sweaty palms and tumbling in his stomach was the same as he remembered. He was nervous about the reception he'd receive after being such a jerk the night before and fully expected a few awkward moments between them when she opened the door.

His sister told him he owed Miz Richmond an apology for his rude attitude, and although the instincts he'd honed the past year rebelled at the thought of groveling for forgiveness, he knew Kristin was right. He'd never treated a woman so shabbily before, and the personal bitterness he harbored was no excuse for his contemptuous behavior.

Shifting on his feet, he cast a surreptitious glance around the small motel parking lot. There were only six units available, and the vacancy sign was still posted. Not many visitors to Cedar Creek required a motel room, so Rafe was fairly certain he'd set a few tongues wagging when he'd entered the registration area and asked Bernice Jones for Lauren Richmond's room number. The old, gray-haired woman had pursed her lips disapprovingly and informed him that she didn't run that kind of establishment. Rafe assured her the visit was strictly business, but that hadn't stopped the old biddy from keeping an eye on him from the glass-enclosed check-in area.

Shoving his misgivings aside, he forced himself to knock on the door. Another thirty seconds passed, which felt like an eternity, then her door opened.

Rafe stared. The polished businesswoman dressed in city sophistication had vanished, and in her place was a young woman with a flush on her cheeks and sleek blond hair pulled into a ponytail. She wore dark blue jeans that gave definition to the curves she'd hidden beneath her fancy suit the night before, and a casual T-shirt hinted at firm, full breasts. She looked pretty and wholesome, like she belonged in Wyoming, in the country...in his bed.

A dazzling smile lit up her face. "Rafe!"

He'd expected reservation or disdain, not such an open display of enthusiasm. "Mornin', Miz Richmond," he drawled, applying a pleasant tone he hadn't used much in the past year. It sounded hoarse and rusty to his ears, but she didn't seem to notice.

She clasped her hands in front of her, nearly bursting with elation. Her gaze searched his, and judging by the excitement electrifying her bluer-than-the-sky-above eyes, he guessed she found what she was looking for.

"You changed your mind!" she blurted.

It wasn't a question, but a statement of fact. One issued with unwavering confidence and complete triumph. He gave a curt nod in response.

With a squeal of delight, she threw herself against his chest, wrapped her arms around his neck and hugged him tighter than he'd ever been embraced before. He tensed, but his discomfort didn't seem to faze her.

"Thank you, thank you, thank you!" she said fervently, her warm breath tickling his ear.

Damn, Rafe thought, overwhelmed by her uninhibited display of gratitude. He didn't know what to do with his hands, so he settled them lightly on her hips, using the strategic placement to maintain a modicum of distance between their bodies. The attempt was no use, not when the woman in his arms clung with such tenacity.

Awareness quickly settled in, stirring senses that had lain dormant for too long. The lush softness of her body complemented his perfectly, making him respond with a rush of heat that spiraled low in his belly, ruthlessly reminding him how long he'd been without a woman. The fresh, feminine scent of her skin filled his head when he pulled in a deep breath. He felt a reckless urge to nuzzle the fragrant curve of her neck and use his tongue to taste the silky, sensitive skin along her throat, to explore the resilience of her supple lips, her mouth, and discover the honeyed essence deep within. To slip his hands around to her bottom and lift her more snugly against him.

Just like that, he wanted her. He craved her warmth and the energy and joy that filled her and surrounded him as she hugged him with such unreserved affection. Emotionally and physically, she made him *feel*, made him need things he'd lost the inclination to care about.

He was in trouble. *Big* trouble. Getting involved with the well-bred, citified Lauren Richmond would only lead to disaster and possible expectations he had no intentions of fulfilling. She didn't seem the type to accept a night of mutual pleasure, no strings attached, and that's all he was willing to offer any woman.

The lecture didn't lessen his desire for her any.

Finally, she let him go, sliding slowly away from the length of his body and creating a sensual friction that had him gritting his teeth.

"Oh, Rafe," she breathed, her eyes as bright as rare jewels. "I can't begin to tell you what this means to me. Chad is going to be absolutely delighted that you're granting his request.''

He was less than thrilled about the situation, but with Kristin's sermon fresh in his mind, he kept the comment to himself. He'd do the deed, albeit reluctantly, then continue on with his quiet, peaceful life.

She stepped back and opened the door wider, motioning him inside. ''Come on in.''

He shook his head and stayed put. ''I don't think that's such a good idea.'' He hooked a finger in the direction of the check-in area, where Bernice watched them with undisguised interest, her brows slanting in a frown. ''Bernice is bound to think something inappropriate is going on.''

Lauren's eyes widened in understanding, and her cheeks colored. ''Oh.'' Her smile turned adorably sheepish. ''I didn't think about how that might look.''

He wasn't surprised, considering where she came from. ''I suppose in Los Angeles people don't pay any attention to such things, but Cedar Creek is a small town, and gossip is a favorite pastime.'' Reaching for a dose of fortitude, he extended a more personal invitation. ''How 'bout I buy you breakfast at Fran's Diner next door, and we can talk there.''

Open pleasure touched her features, matching the smile that curved her mouth. ''I'd like that, but I've got to be on the road in about an hour to catch my flight back to Los Angeles.''

He glanced at his watch, noted the time and mentally counted the minutes until he'd be at his ranch with his horses. ''That won't be a problem.''

He waited outside while she grabbed her purse, and together they walked to the diner. Lauren gave

Bernice a friendly wave on the way. The old woman appeared flustered at being caught watching them and quickly busied herself at the registration desk.

Since it was late morning on a Wednesday, the place wasn't very busy, though the few patrons tracked their progress to a booth in the back of the establishment. Not only was it a novelty to see Rafe Dalton out in public for something other than groceries or a trip to the feed store, but the unfamiliar woman he was with heightened their curiosity.

Rafe retrieved two plastic menus from between the salt and pepper shakers and napkin dispenser and handed one to Lauren. Out of the corner of his eye, he could see their waitress sashaying her way to their table. He recognized her as Andrea Ferris, one of the many women who'd traipsed through his house when he'd come home after the accident, trying to take care of him and fuss over his injuries when he didn't want anyone near him. He'd been filled with anger, and surly enough to offend many of the women he'd grown up with—women who'd tried for years to catch his eye and rope him into a commitment he wasn't ready for, Andrea included. Shortly, the visits stopped and word quickly spread that Rafe Dalton was no longer the sweet-talking charmer he'd been since his youth.

She stopped at their table, pencil and tablet in hand, and gave him a slow, thorough once-over. "Well, what a surprise it is to see you here, Rafe."

He gave her a curt nod. "Hello, Andrea."

The woman's green, catlike eyes slid from him to Lauren and back again. "Who's your friend?"

Belatedly, Rafe realized the mistake in bringing Lauren here, which put her, and him, under as much scrutiny as if he'd entered her motel room. In his estimation, it wasn't anyone's business who Lauren was or what she was doing in Cedar Creek. The last thing he wanted was the town having a field day with what he'd agreed to do for Lauren.

Both women waited for an introduction, and when he didn't issue one, Lauren took the initiative. "I'm Lauren Richmond," she said with a congenial smile. "I'm from Los Angeles."

"Really?" Intrigue suffused Andrea's voice. "What brings you to a town like Cedar Creek?"

"I represent Bright Beginnings, which caters to foster children," Lauren said, before Rafe could formulate an excuse for her visit. "I have a client who wants to meet Rafe. He's agreed, so now we're hashing out some details."

"Ah, who can resist Cedar Creek's rodeo champion and local hero?" Andrea's comment spilled out with a sarcastic bite, and she shifted her gaze to Rafe. "What you're doing is just too sweet for words, darlin'. It's nice to know there's still a gracious side to you, after all." She followed that remark with a question. "So, what can I get you two today?"

Rafe was grateful for the change in conversation, especially since Lauren looked totally confused by the exchange between him and Andrea. It was obvious his unsociable attitude the past year hadn't won him any popularity votes. Once, he'd been well-liked and respected in Cedar Creek. Now the people of the community treated him like they did his father when he'd been alive—civilly, but not making any attempt to breach the hostility he'd cloaked himself in since the accident.

It was his own fault, but the knowledge that he

was becoming exactly what he'd always despised was a tough pill to swallow.

"I'll have the ham and cheese omelette with white toast," he told Andrea, not looking at her. Setting the menu aside, he looked out the window to the Lazy Daze motel while Lauren placed her order.

"I'll have the same," she said. "And I'll take cream with my coffee, please."

Andrea wrote the order on her pad. "Coming right up."

Once they were alone, Rafe glanced at Lauren and found her regarding him with concern. He instantly felt uneasy.

"Are you okay?" she asked quietly.

Why did she care? "Just fine." A tight smile stretched his lips. He wasn't about to admit just how uncomfortable this situation was making him.

Andrea returned with her coffeepot and two mugs. She set the mugs on the table, along with a container of cream, and filled both cups with steaming brew, then moved on to another table to take a customer's order. Rafe swallowed his stubborn, irritable pride and attempted to make amends for his behavior the evening before.

"I, uh, owe you an apology for last night." He could have made the excuse that she'd caught him at a bad time, but didn't. More often than not, his mood was as dark and ominous as a thundercloud.

She waved a slim hand in the air, dismissing the incident. "I think both of us were a little short-tempered yesterday. I was tired and cranky after my long flight and probably came on stronger than I normally would have." Her expression filled with warmth and understanding. "Why don't we wipe the slate clean and start out fresh?"

"All right." His reply was stiff with a reluctance he couldn't shake. "So what, exactly, do you expect from me in all this?"

"To be hospitable, if that's a possibility." Her tone was light and teasing, but underlined with honesty, too. She stirred cream into her coffee and added a packet of sugar. "That scowl of yours is enough to make a young kid cower."

He braced his forearms on the table, clasped his hands around his mug and tried to relax his facial muscles so he was no longer glowering. The technique took more effort than he'd expected and made him think about how a scowl had become such a natural form of expression for him. *She* made him think too much.

"Entertaining kids isn't my specialty," he said, his voice low and defensive.

"You entertained hundreds of kids during your rodeo days," she pointed out, a sassy grin curving her mouth. "And according to Chad, you were quite amicable about it, too."

"Yeah, well, things have a tendency to change." A gruff note infused his voice. He took a drink of coffee to ease the roughness. "I don't follow the circuit any longer, and I don't make it a habit of turning my spread into a dude ranch for some kid with a hankering to play cowboy."

"I'm not asking you to change your daily routine, just give a little time to a young boy." A wisp of hair had escaped her ponytail, and she took a moment to tuck it behind her ear. "When Chad's father was alive he took him to a working ranch a few times, so he knows what to expect. He's taking riding lessons and is quite adept with horses. And he'll be chaperoned, so it's not as though he'll be in your way while you're working."

"His foster parents are coming, too?"

"Well, no, not exactly." She absently fiddled with her fork and knife, but her gaze remained focused on him. "Both of them work and can't take the time off. Since I've accumulated vacation time at Blair, I offered to chaperone him during his stay and be his guardian for the week."

A rumble of heat coursed through Rafe's blood that had nothing to do with the hot coffee he'd just swallowed. He thought about seven days of this woman living in his house, sleeping in the spare bedroom next to his, leaving her scent in every room she entered, and wondered how he'd survive when she already proved to be a temptation he was hard-pressed to resist.

She brought her mug to her lips and took a sip of the sweetened brew, suddenly looking uncertain. "Your, um, girlfriend won't mind us staying at your place, will she?"

Her question caught him by surprise, and it took him a moment to figure out a response. Eyeing her cautiously, he asked, "What gives you the idea I have a girlfriend?"

She shifted against the vinyl booth. As uncomfortable as she appeared, that determination he was coming to admire fueled her gaze. "Yesterday, when I knocked on your door you thought I was Kristin."

Her conclusion nearly caused him to smile. He caught it just in time. "Kristin is my sister. I have no doubt you'll meet her during your stay."

She breathed a sigh of relief, her shoulders visibly relaxing. "Oh, good. I'm glad I won't have to worry about a girlfriend." A startled look crossed her features, as if she realized how forward her comment sounded. "I mean, it's not as though I don't *want* you to have a girlfriend, I just wouldn't want to cause any problems...."

He decided to save her before she completely embarrassed herself. "I understand."

Andrea delivered their omelettes and toast, then addressed Lauren with a friendly smile, blatantly ignoring Rafe. "I was just telling Fran what you're doing for that kid, and she said to make sure you bring the boy by for breakfast one morning for her special banana pecan pancakes, on the house."

"That's awfully nice. Thank you." Lauren beamed delightedly at the kind gesture Andrea had just extended. "I'll be sure to do that."

Andrea topped off their mugs with fresh, hot coffee, not in any hurry to move on to her other customers. "So, you'll be staying out at Rafe's?"

"Yes." Lauren cast Rafe a casual glance as if to assess how much to reveal, but he knew his carefully blank expression offered her no answers. So she formulated her own. "Rafe thought it would be more convenient if Chad and I stayed at his place, instead of the motel, so that way he can spend more time with Chad."

He inwardly cringed, wishing he *had* offered a more vague explanation. Her lie gave too much credence to the hero he wasn't.

"Really?" Andrea's brows rose in flagrant disbelief. "I didn't know Rafe had a soft spot for kids, or anything else, for that matter."

"Oh, Rafe has been absolutely wonderful about all this," Lauren embellished, leaving the other woman speechless.

"Andrea, order up!" the cook called, saving all of them from further lies or cutting remarks.

Andrea gave Rafe one last look, as if seeing him in a different light, then headed behind the counter to deliver her orders.

Rafe reached for the bottle of ketchup, then poured the sauce over his crisp hash browns. "That wasn't necessary."

Lauren cut off a piece of omelette and stabbed it with her fork. "It was if you want to do something about that nasty reputation of yours."

Irritation touched his nerves, and he glared at her over his breakfast. "My reputation is none of your business."

Her chin came up. "It is when I have a young client to think about." She shot the words back.

"If you'll recall, *I* didn't ask for any of this." His tone was low and heated. How was it that this woman had the ability to push his hottest, most temperamental buttons?

She stared at him for long seconds, the fire in her eyes gradually fading to a pale blue. "No, you didn't," she admitted quietly, though she didn't call off the arrangement, like he half-hoped she would. Instead, she picked up her knife and calmly slathered grape jelly on her toast. "Tell me something, Rafe. If you're so against Chad and his request, what changed your mind?"

"My sister."

"You're doing this for her?"

"I'm doing it for the boy. My sister reminded me

of how we felt when we lost our mother when we were kids.''

Gentle compassion reflected on her face. "I'm sorry.''

He shrugged and finished chewing his bite of omelette. "It was a long time ago, but the confusion and fears we experienced are probably the same thing Chad is going through." Before she had a chance to ask about his father, who was also dead, he added, "Personally, I'm against this entire farce."

She stiffened, the gesture defensive and challenging. "What do you mean, 'farce'?"

He set down his fork and looked her straight in the eye, his mouth grim. "Chad expects a rodeo cowboy, Lauren. I don't even ride anymore, not like he remembers or expects me to. Some days I'm in agony after riding a sweet, gentle mare for an hour." Bitterness crept into his voice, and he struggled to keep it from spoiling the conversation. "I'm not the champion bull rider he remembers. And the last thing I want to do is offer this kid any false hopes."

Spontaneously, she reached across the table and laid her hand on his arm. He felt that touch all the way to his cold, empty soul, and wished for a moment that this woman with the sky-blue eyes and soft-looking lips didn't live in such a drastically different world than his own.

Her gaze implored him to understand, to compromise. "Is it too much to ask that you be Chad's friend for a week? Right now, more than a champion bull rider, he needs someone to accept him unconditionally, and you're the one he's chosen."

He felt himself softening. Relenting. "You don't ask for much, do you?"

She grinned, her eyes alight with mischief. "Tell you what, Rafe, I'll make you a deal. If you can be Chad's buddy for a week and make him feel a little bit special, then I promise not to tell anyone here in Cedar Creek just how nice you really are."

She winked at him, as if it would be their secret, and he had to bite the inside of his cheek to keep from chuckling. That she had the ability to evoke amusement in him was as startling as it was invigorating.

On the heels of that revelation came a more troubling thought. He had an uneasy feeling that once Lauren Richmond blew through his life, the solitary world he'd created for himself would never be the same again.

CHAPTER THREE

Two weeks later, on a Friday afternoon, Lauren drove a rental car from Cody to Cedar Creek, this time with Chad Evans as her companion. The windows were rolled down, allowing the clean, country air to circulate through the vehicle and whip through their hair. The blue sky stretching endlessly in front of them was a welcome change from the hot, smog-filled air they'd left behind in Los Angeles.

"Are we almost there?" an anxious voice asked.

Lauren glanced at the young boy sitting in the passenger seat. His blond hair was rumpled from the breeze, and his big brown eyes contained an infectious excitement. The huge grin on his face seemed permanent, which made Lauren extremely grateful Rafe had agreed to spend time with him. The memories Chad collected in the next week would go a long way in restoring his self-confidence and would bring a bit of happiness to his lonely life.

"About another ten minutes and we'll be in Cedar Creek," she said, sending a warm smile his way. "But before we get to Rafe's, I'd like to stop and pick up some extra groceries, so Rafe won't have to worry about meals while we're here."

A flicker of disappointment crossed his features, but he didn't verbally express it. Instead, he chewed on his bottom lip. "He knows we're coming, right?"

So many worries for someone so young. "Yeah,

Rafe knows we're coming. I left a message for him with his sister to expect us sometime this afternoon.''

Seeming satisfied with her answer, he turned his attention to the open window and the farms and ranches dotting the countryside.

The town of Cedar Creek was just as hospitable and receptive as Kristin had been on the phone, Lauren discovered when they stopped at the local market ten minutes later. By the time they finished picking up groceries for the week, the checker, box boy and manager of the store knew who they were and why they were in Cedar Creek.

Finally, after a stop at the gas station to fill up their empty tank, they drove to the dirt road that led to Rafe's spread.

''Wow, look at all those horses,'' Chad exclaimed, his gaze riveted to the dozen or more chestnuts grazing in the fenced-in pasture. ''Do you think he'll let me ride one?''

Lauren parked the sedan next to Rafe's truck. ''Oh, I'm sure he will.''

''Cool!'' Chad unhooked his seat belt, jammed his pint-size black Stetson on his head and scrambled from the car. Skipping enthusiastically, he headed toward a corral confining two mares and their foals.

Lauren followed at a more leisurely pace, enjoying Chad's excitement and energy after enduring a five-hour plane ride, then being cooped up for two hours in a car. At the fence, Chad stood on the second rung to gently pet the mare that ambled up to the railing for attention.

''Isn't she just the prettiest thing you've ever seen?'' Chad asked, rubbing the docile horse along her nose.

The mare's chestnut coat gleamed with health, and her big, dark eyes seem to contain a smile. "She's absolutely beautiful," Lauren agreed, stroking the horse's neck. "And friendly, too."

Lauren glanced around for Rafe while Chad lavished the mare with praise, but the ranch was quiet and peaceful. Just when she thought she'd have to go searching for their host, he exited one of the stables, saw them and headed their way in a slow, lazy stroll that belied the slight hitch in his walk.

Something deep within Lauren's breast fluttered. Dressed in a dusty pair of jeans, a chambray shirt cuffed to his elbows and leather boots that appeared well broken in, he looked like he'd put in a hard day's work. Today, he wore a black Stetson identical to Chad's.

His eyes were shaded by the brim of his hat, but she sensed the sweep of his gaze taking in her cool summer outfit, down her long bare legs to the strappy sandals on her feet. The corner of his lips twitched in the barest of smiles, as if he appreciated what he saw. If she hadn't been staring at his mouth, she would have missed that very subtle response.

Awareness swirled through her, tying her stomach in knots and making her skin tingle and tighten. She'd never been attracted to the dark, ominous type, but there was something about Rafe Dalton that made her pulse quicken, made her wonder if those chiseled lips of his ever relaxed with laughter. She wondered if he'd kiss as hard and abrupt as his manners, or if his mouth softened and gentled when it claimed a woman's—turned slow, thorough and sensual.

Stopping a few feet away, he tipped his hat at her. "Lauren," he acknowledged pleasantly, a direct contrast to the man who'd greeted her the last time she'd been on his ranch. "Nice to see you again."

His voice was a low, husky rumble that stroked her senses. She didn't know if he was just being polite, or if he really meant it. A wry smile lifted the corner of her mouth. "It's nice to see you, too."

He turned his attention to Chad, who'd jumped down from the fence railing and stared at him with huge, round eyes.

"Hello, pardner," Rafe drawled.

Chad swallowed. "Hello, Mr. Dalton." His voice quavered with nerves, and in an attempt to make a favorable impression, he thrust his hand out for Rafe to shake. "Thank you for letting me visit and stay on your ranch."

Chad sounded so formal and grown up it was all Lauren could do to suppress a smile.

"You're welcome." Rafe clasped his hand and gave it a firm, masculine shake. "And why don't you call me Rafe?"

Chad beamed, his grin brighter than pure sunshine. "Okay...Rafe."

Rafe ran his finger along the brim of Chad's Stetson. "Mighty fine-looking hat you got yourself there."

Chad's cheeks colored, and he ducked his head sheepishly. "It's just like yours."

"I'm very flattered." There was a gentle, affable note to Rafe's voice that made Chad look up. "It's just the kind of hat you'll need to keep the sun out of your eyes while you're working and riding the range."

Chad straightened like a little soldier who'd been

assigned a special mission. "I'll work real hard for you, Rafe," he promised solemnly.

Rafe gave him a nod of acceptance, then glanced at Lauren. She knew how difficult this was for Rafe, and she hoped her gaze conveyed just how much she appreciated his kindness and patience with Chad.

"Why don't we go and get your things unloaded and into the house?" he suggested.

"That would be fine." She smiled. "I bought some groceries, too."

Together, they worked to unload the sedan, bringing in the luggage and toting the sacks of food to the kitchen. Rafe put their suitcases in the only spare room in the house and told Chad he could camp out on the couch, which thrilled the young boy.

While Chad ate a light snack of apple juice and oatmeal raisin cookies and talked to Rafe about the riding lessons he'd taken, Lauren put away the groceries. Before long, they were done, with Chad eager to head outside and explore.

Everything had gone smoother than Lauren had expected. Rafe was being congenial and friendly and not exhibiting any resentment for the intrusion into his private life. Strolling beside Chad as Rafe explained the layout of the ranch, Lauren was beginning to think everything was going to be just fine...until a beige sedan crested the dirt hill and pulled up in front of Rafe's house.

Rafe must have recognized the visitor, because he froze mid-speech and mid-stroll, though Chad skipped ahead to a pen housing a few goats. Lauren stopped, too, sensing a change in Rafe's disposition. A young, good-looking man wearing a shirt, tie and slacks climbed from the driver's side of the car and waved at them.

Rafe glanced sharply at her, the censure in his gaze chilling her to the bone. His voice was low and edged in steel when he spoke. "What the *hell* is the editor of the local paper doing here?"

The heat and animosity radiating off Rafe startled her, as did the blatant accusation he cast her way. Before she could respond to his fierce demand, the man approaching them issued an answer.

"Hey, Rafe, I heard about the kid and his request to meet you and thought it would make a great human-interest article for the Cedar Creek *Gazette*." His drawl was rich with sarcasm. "Everybody loves a local hero, and this is just too interesting a piece to pass up."

Rafe's entire body tensed, and a muscle in his lean jaw ticked. "There isn't a story for you here, Jason." The warning vibrating in his voice was unmistakable.

Jason chose to ignore Rafe's unwelcome statement. "Sure, there is," he said, flashing a dazzling grin Lauren's way that belied the tenacity in his gaze. "The entire town is all abuzz about your generous offer to entertain this foster child. You have to admit this is quite a surprise, considering what a recluse you've been this past year."

"What I do, and for what reasons, is nobody's business but my own," Rafe responded succinctly, proving more obstinate than the adversary he faced. "Find yourself another story. And the next time you ignore that No Trespassing sign posted out front, I'll be pressing charges."

Sparing Lauren a glance that spoke volumes of anger and frustration, Rafe turned and stalked away, favoring his right leg. With a sinking feeling in her stomach, she watched him head toward where Chad was playing with the goats and chickens. She was relieved to see Rafe tug playfully on the brim of Chad's Stetson as he talked to the boy. At least Rafe's animosity didn't extend to Chad.

"The man certainly knows how to pour on the charm, doesn't he?" Jason reflected with cynical humor.

"You know, this really isn't a good time for an interview," she said, returning her attention to the man beside her. "Chad and I just arrived, and we're exhausted from the long trip. We'll be here for the next week, so maybe you could do this another time?" Like after she discovered why Rafe was so opposed to an interview that would do more good for his reputation and Bright Beginnings than harm.

"You ready for bed, sleepyhead?" Lauren asked Chad, ruffling his hair affectionately.

"Yeah," he admitted sheepishly, not bothering to smother his tired yawn.

It was nine o'clock, and the day's excitement had taken its toll on Chad. She helped him get ready for bed and situated him on the couch. Within minutes, the boy was fast asleep. The house grew quiet, and Lauren headed to the guest bedroom to unpack, then took a quick shower and changed into her favorite cotton jersey nightshirt.

As much as she wanted to talk to Rafe about this afternoon's incident with Jason, he'd made it difficult for her to accomplish her goal by avoiding being alone with her for the rest of the afternoon and evening. He remained warm and friendly with Chad, who'd blossomed from Rafe's attention as they continued their tour of the ranch. As for her, he'd been civil and polite when the need arose to address her, but there was no escaping the more resentful emotions simmering in his steel-gray eyes when he looked at her.

Even now, he was sequestered somewhere on his expansive ranch, avoiding her, no doubt. Well, she planned to wait him out.

Determined to resolve the tension between them tonight so they'd have a chance of a pleasant week together, she grabbed the novel she'd started reading on the flight to Wyoming, crawled into bed and immersed herself in the romantic suspense. The next thing she knew she'd dozed off, and it was Rafe's heavy booted steps coming down the hall that woke her. By the time she'd scrambled out of bed and opened her door, he was already in his room, which was next to hers. She heard his shower come on before she could knock.

Blowing out an aggravated stream of breath, she braced her back against the wall next to the door and waited. Another ten minutes, and she heard him moving around in his room. A drawer opened and closed. She gave him time to get dressed, then knocked lightly.

"Yeah?"

His rough and sexy voice strummed along feminine nerves, causing her pulse to quicken—with nerves or excitement, she wasn't sure. She shifted on her bare feet and forced out her request before she changed her mind. "I was wondering if we could talk."

He hesitated so long, she began to think he wasn't

going to answer or planned to refuse her. Finally, he said, "Come on in."

She opened the door and stepped into his domain, then instantly realized her mistake in being so bold. He stood in the center of the large room, surrounded by dark wood furnishings that matched his personality. He was casually tying the drawstring on his cotton sweat shorts. His black hair was damp and finger combed away from his face, his lips firm and unyielding, his muscular chest bare. Though she'd seen him without a shirt before, the sight of all that rugged, masculine perfection was no less breathtaking than the first time she'd laid eyes on those wide shoulders and washboard lean belly. His brazen disregard for his lack of attire was as reckless and daring as the glint in his eyes, sparking lush, vibrant sensations deep within her.

She drew a breath to regain her composure and inhaled the warm, clean scent that clung to him in the aftermath of his shower. Heat and unwanted desire curled low in her belly, spreading outward, making her too aware of the intimacy of the situation. Making her too aware of this man's sex appeal and magnetism, despite his brooding attitude.

What had she been thinking to barge into his room? In an attempt to right her wrong, she blurted, "Could we do it in the kitchen?"

The slight curving of his lips mocked her, as did the gray eyes that leisurely drifted the length of her, lingering a tad too long, and with too much interest, on the bare legs that extended from the hem of her sleep shirt. "We can do it anywhere you like."

His double entendre wasn't lost on her, or the fact that he was trying to intimidate her. But she wasn't easily threatened by a man who seemed to be more growl than bite.

"I mean *talk*," she explained.

His gaze flickered to hers, filled with a brash and reckless insolence. "I never thought differently," he drawled.

She didn't believe the rogue for a second. For some reason, he was feeling defensive about today's incident and was clearly trying to provoke her into letting the entire episode pass without reconciling anything between them.

Not a chance, Mr. Three-time PRCA Rodeo Champion, she thought. She planned to ride this particular bull for the eight seconds required to score a victory.

With that bit of tenacity firmly established in her mind, she turned and crossed quietly through the living room, where Chad was sleeping peacefully, to the kitchen.

She flipped the light switch on the wall and waited for her ornery bull to arrive behind her.

Rafe followed Lauren at a slower pace, the ache in his right thigh a constant, nagging reminder of why he'd chosen a solitary life. Now this woman was wreaking havoc with his quiet, secluded existence and dragging the townsfolk of Cedar Creek into his private business. One day, and she was turning his life upside down and provoking him in ways that he didn't want to acknowledge or analyze, stimulating emotions he'd thought himself no longer capable of feeling.

He entered the kitchen, scowl in place. She wasn't affected by his fierce expression or his boorish attitude, which annoyed him all the more, because he found her obstinate nature a tempting challenge.

She stood by the counter waiting patiently for him. Arms folded over her chest and features determinedly set, she looked as stubborn as she was beautiful. And she was beautiful, even with her face freshly scrubbed and wearing an old, faded sleep shirt. He'd expected silk and lace from her, but she was proving to be more substance than frills. More practical than predictable...another trait he found too damn appealing.

Grabbing a chair, he spun it around, straddled the seat and rested his arms along the back. "The floor is all yours, Miz Richmond," he said.

Her eyes flashed fire over the impertinent way he rolled her last name on his tongue, but she kept her irritation tamped. "I want to apologize about this afternoon and for the gentleman from the Cedar Creek *Gazette* showing up like he did."

"I agreed to let Chad stay here for a week," he said. "I didn't agree to a field day with the local paper."

Her eyes widened a fraction. "You think *I* set up that interview?"

He lifted a brow. "Didn't you?"

She stiffened indignantly and pursed her lips. "No, I didn't. I can't help it if the people in town are curious about you granting a foster child's special request. What you're doing for Chad is unique, and certainly charitable enough to pique human interest."

"I don't appreciate having my privacy invaded."

"Whether you believe it or not, I respect your privacy," she retorted, exasperated. "But I don't understand what is so bad about people hearing what you're doing for Chad and Bright Beginnings.''

''It's none of their business!'' Too late, he realized his tone was so harsh it prompted Lauren to regard him speculatively, her gaze searching past barriers he'd erected the past year. The urge to bolt was strong, overwhelming almost, but he remained sitting, glaring at her, unwavering.

After a long-drawn-out moment, she sighed as if to release some tension and dragged her fingers through her silky hair. The shimmering warmth beckoned his fingertips, made him wonder what the luxurious mass would feel like crushed in his hands, what her hair would smell like if he got close enough to breathe in that scent. He imagined the fragrance of sunshine and wildflowers and realized how long it had been since he'd appreciated such sweet, wholesome scents…and how badly he craved those essential, sensual indulgences with her.

She tilted her head, her eyes a calming shade of blue. ''What are you hiding from, Rafe?'' she asked softly.

Her perception made him uneasy and forced him to think about a part of his life he'd left behind, the wrong choices he was ashamed of, the many mistakes he'd made. ''I don't know what you're talking about.'' He stood and headed toward the refrigerator, ignoring the stiffness that had settled in his thigh.

''Don't you?'' She watched him grab a can of soda, open it and take a long drink. When the silence stretched between them with no answer from him, she continued. ''For the past two months, every time Chad has brought you up, he's talked about a fun-loving, carefree cowboy who wowed the crowds with his charm and gave of himself so selflessly to his fans. Where is that man?''

''He no longer exists,'' he said, his tone as flat and emotionless as he suddenly felt.

''Is that why there isn't a trace of that three-time PRCA bull-riding champion in this house?'' she asked, slowly closing the distance between them. ''There's no trophies, no plaques, nothing to indicate that you led an invigorating, exciting life before your accident.''

''None of those material things matter.''

She frowned as if she didn't understand. ''Those things are a part of your past and who you are.''

He laughed, the sound harsh and humorless. ''This is who I am, Lauren. A simple cowboy who raises Quarter Horses and doesn't like the fact that his life has been pried open for public speculation.''

''Why?'' she persisted. ''Are you afraid that people are going to see a caring side to you, which is going to totally shatter their illusion of the surly man you pretend to be so no one will try to get too close?''

''Leave it alone, Lauren.'' Finished with his drink, and more than through with their conversation, he crushed the aluminum can, tossed it into the trash and moved around her.

''I have no idea why you're so bitter, or why you chose to alienate yourself from the people of Cedar Creek, but don't expect me to cater to that illusion,'' she said, stopping him in his slow progress. She waited for him to turn around, then allowed a satisfied smile to curve her lips. ''I call the shots as I see them, Rafe, and even though you want everyone to believe you've become this awful person, I know you're a good, kind man.''

He pointed a finger at her, fury mixing with an inexplicable need to believe her words. He embraced the first emotion, which was easier for him to accept. ''You know *nothing* about me.''

Her chin jutted out mutinously. ''I know you're a hero who feels burdened by the honorary title, resents it, even.''

He bristled, and it took monumental effort for him to keep his voice from exploding with the anger that gripped him. ''I never asked to be a hero, and I certainly didn't do anything to deserve the title!''

''Except save another person's life,'' she retorted with dry sarcasm. ''That's about as heroic as it gets.''

His insides twisted relentlessly, the truth burning in his stomach like acid. If she only knew just how responsible he'd been for the tragedy that had taken place, she wouldn't be so staunch in supporting him. But as much as he knew the truth would shock her and serve as the barrier he needed to distance himself from this woman, he couldn't bring himself to say the incriminating words out loud.

Frustrated at her zealous quest to portray him as a kind, compassionate man when he wanted no part of her fanciful notions, he grabbed her arm and tugged her close, intending to frighten her enough that she'd back off and leave him alone. The unexpected move threw her off balance, and she stumbled forward. Her hands automatically shot out and landed on his chest. Her cool palms on his tight, heated skin sent a jolt through him.

She appeared startled, but not at all alarmed by his rough handling, which only served to spike his temper another notch. He leaned close. His face was inches from hers, so close that the feminine scent he'd imagined only moments before turned to drugging reality, so close that he witnessed the darkening of her eyes, the unconscious parting of her lips.

"You think I'm heroic?" he asked in a low, ferocious growl that rumbled in his chest. "Just for the record, darlin', I don't have a chivalrous bone in my entire body. I don't give a damn about anything or anyone but myself."

She dampened her bottom lip with her tongue, her eyes locked on his. Her body relaxed, flowing toward his until her thighs brushed sensually against his and the tips of her breasts grazed his chest, beckoning his baser male desires. Slowly, she stroked a hand upward, trailing her fingers over his shoulder, then settled them along the curve of his neck. An impudent light entered her gaze, and she smiled, of all things!

"I don't believe you," she whispered.

His jaw tightened at the gentleness of her touch. His heart rebelled at the care in her eyes, neither of which he'd asked for or wanted.

"You don't believe I'm the worst kind of bastard?" She didn't respond to his challenge, but the dare in her eyes spoke volumes. She silently rebuked his judgmental claim, candidly invited the trouble that brewed between them with the intensity of a summer storm.

The raging tempest within him gathered momentum, clashing with the tenderness she offered and the self-recriminations he'd cloaked himself in the past year. Refusing to allow this woman to breach those boundaries, unwilling to let her think he was in any way virtuous or benevolent, he clung to the black reputation he'd earned.

In a quick, dizzying movement, he maneuvered her back three steps until her spine flattened against the cool enamel refrigerator door and his hard, muscular body pressed intimately into her soft, lush curves. His chest crushed her full breasts, his belly aligned with hers, and one hard, hair-roughened thigh slipped between her slender, smooth legs. He trapped her with his superior strength, surrounding them both in a heat greater than pure fire. She sucked in a surprised breath but didn't attempt to push him away or struggle, didn't even issue a token protest.

He buried his hands in her sleek hair, unable to resist the feel of those silken strands twining around his fingers, tormenting himself with what he knew he'd never have for more than this moment. He tilted her face toward his, tried desperately not to lose himself in her soft, beguiling gaze, and summoned the gruffest voice he could manage. "If you don't believe I'm the worst kind of bastard, then let me prove it."

He dropped his mouth over hers, bypassing any of the cajoling, tender preliminaries of a first kiss and going straight to the heart of the matter. His lips melded with hers, hot and insistent. His tongue was just as relentless, gaining entrance and gliding deeply, more possessively than he'd ever branded a woman.

He expected outrage for his audacity, at the very least resistance. He certainly deserved a severe lash of fury for being so brazen. But instead of shoving him away like he half-wished she would, she tentatively slid her palm around the nape of his neck and pulled him closer, if that was possible.

Oh, yeah, it was possible. Her fingers sieved through his damp hair, and her spine curved toward his until it was impossible to distinguish where his body ended and hers began. Her mouth was warm and giving beneath the onslaught of his, and so damned tempting he lost track of his original purpose. And since it had been forever since he'd kissed a woman, and never one quite so guileless and trusting, he greedily took what she so selflessly offered—salvation.

She moaned softly, sweetly, and stroked her tongue along his. Her breasts swelled, and he could feel her nipples tighten against his chest through her thin cotton nightshirt. Her response was honest and real, and that open vulnerability completely unraveled him.

What had begun as a punishment she turned into a seduction of wills. Anger melted into a hunger and need he'd denied himself for far too long. Pain turned to undeniable pleasure. With a touch, a kiss, she awakened the primal male animal in him, made him feel alive and whole.

A heavy, aching desire rushed through his veins, warning him where this interlude was headed if he didn't cut it off at the pass—and fast! Lauren didn't seem to fear any repercussions, or maybe she trusted him to halt their tryst before it spiraled out of control. The little fool. If only she knew he was seconds away from hauling her over his shoulder and carrying her to his bed so he could lose himself in the softness of her body, the all-consuming redemption of her touch.

Furious with himself for letting things go so far,

equally incensed at her for making him *feel*, he lifted his mouth from hers and took a step away from her alluring body, her bewitching stare.

She leaned against the refrigerator, her hands pressed to the sides as if for support. Her breathing was just as ragged as his, her lips wet and swollen, her blue eyes dazed and smoky with desire. So much for scaring her off, he thought irritably.

And then, as he watched, an intuitive, womanly smile flirted around the corners of her mouth, then fully developed. "The only thing you proved is that you're an incredible kisser," she said with husky assurance, "and a man who needs a little tenderness and understanding."

Anger swept through him once more, and he narrowed his gaze on her, holding fast to mockery. "And you think you're that person?"

She didn't answer his question, but he didn't need a verbal response to validate the astute patience and feminine wisdom glimmering in her eyes—a keen knowledge that shook him to the core, especially after what had just transpired between them.

"Don't fool yourself, Lauren," he replied with a forced calm he was far from experiencing. "I'm not a man you can depend on, and I don't offer commitments and promises in exchange for a little tenderness and understanding. Save it for the foster kids you work with, because they need it more than I do."

Before he said or did something else he regretted, Rafe left the kitchen—and Lauren—and returned to his bedroom alone.

Sleep was a long time coming.

CHAPTER FOUR

WARM streams of sunshine filtered through the bedroom window, touching Lauren's face, gently beckoning her to awaken. She resisted, indulging in the languor infusing her limbs and the wonderful dreams wisping through her mind—visions of a man with dark hair, striking gray eyes and the ability to make her body and soul come alive with a kiss....

The image faded, and as much as she struggled to hold on to it, reality insisted on rudely intruding, forcing her to awaken. Opening her eyes, she stretched lazily, then reached for the watch she'd put on the nightstand. She was shocked to discover it was after eleven Wyoming time. Usually her internal alarm clock woke her at six, and she was dressed and ready to face the day by seven. Then again, she usually slept restfully, whereas last night she'd tossed and turned until the early hours of the morning, compliments of one moody, temperamental cowboy. Never had a man totally consumed her thoughts, her dreams. Then again, no other man had ever awakened such deep desires with such an emotional, needy embrace—one she found both scary and exhilarating.

Unfortunately, he refused to acknowledge the same awesome need, choosing instead to cling to whatever dark demons drove him. His gruff, intimidating act didn't fool her. She'd tasted the raw hunger in his kiss, had witnessed the torment in his eyes and knew he struggled to fight the awareness between them, the craving for a deeper union, and most especially the tenderness and care she offered.

Stubborn, cantankerous man!

Sighing softly and admitting temporary defeat, she listened for sounds in the house. Hearing none, she surmised both Chad and Rafe had awakened hours ago and were most likely out on the ranch somewhere. And since she'd slept nearly half the day away, she needed to get up and join them—despite her host's attempt to keep his distance. First and foremost, she had a client to chaperone, and she was determined to ensure Chad had a good time during his vacation.

Half an hour later, after changing into a pair of jeans and a ribbed T-shirt and eating a quick breakfast of cereal and a bran muffin, she ventured outside.

The beautiful Saturday morning was unlike anything California had to offer. She was used to dingy smog polluting the air. The vast Wyoming sky was cloudless and so blindingly blue it seemed to stretch for eternity. Birds twittered in nearby trees. Their chatter was broken by a soft neigh of a horse or the squabble of chickens hashing over a kernel of food. The calm and tranquillity of the country were so different from the obnoxious city sounds she was used to. She loved the serenity, the slow pace and the wholesomeness that surrounded her. A mild breeze, fragrant with the scent of grass and more earthy elements, drifted through her unbound hair, reminding her of the way Rafe's fingers had tangled through the strands last night. The sensual memory curled through her, and she resolutely dismissed the luxurious thought before it escalated.

She had little reason to worry about Chad's welfare. She found her young wannabe cowboy in a corral under a shady awning, standing next to Rafe and a docile mare they were in the process of saddling. Since the two seemed intent on their task—with Rafe instructing and Chad listening and complying with Rafe's directions—Lauren quietly sidled up to the split-rail fence enclosing the pen and watched them work together.

Observing Rafe was certainly no hardship. He had a backside she could admire for hours. Broad shoulders sloped down a well-defined back, tapering into a trim waist and lean hips. Soft, faded denim molded his buttocks and clung to muscular thighs. Though each movement he made was fluid and economical, his entire body was a package of concentrated power and strength that belied the gentle way he stroked his long fingers down the chestnut's neck and the soft way he crooned to the mare while Chad buckled the girth. She found Rafe incredibly sexy when he wasn't pretending his fierce warrior routine.

A soft, appreciative sigh escaped her, ending on a tiny hum of pleasure that tickled her throat. The unintentional sound caught Rafe's attention, and he glanced over his shoulder, his gaze colliding with hers.

He wasn't wearing his Stetson—sheltered from the sun, he didn't need one. His thick, black hair was combed away from his face, layering softly on the sides and falling along his T-shirt in the back. The style accentuated the lean lines of his cheeks, nose and jaw and drew attention to his lips, which had lost their hard edge and appeared full, soft and giving.

Something deep within her belly fluttered, warm and exciting.

The harsh expression that had lined his features the previous evening was gone, replaced by a slight, uncertain frown. Wariness shone in his pewter eyes, along with a good dose of reservation. His stance had turned rigid upon seeing her, cautious, but she saw no trace of last night's brash attitude.

She offered him a smile.

He didn't return it, though he inclined his head ever so slightly in greeting. ''Morning,'' he murmured, his voice a rich rumble of sound.

She wondered if his manners were for Chad's benefit. If it wasn't for her young foster client, she was certain Rafe would have sent her packing last night. ''Good morning, Rafe,'' she said brightly, determined to keep things amicable between them.

Chad poked his head around the horse, a huge grin on his face. ''Hi, Lauren!'' he said exuberantly, full of life and energy. ''I guess you were the sleepyhead this morning, huh?''

''Yeah, I guess I was,'' she admitted with light laughter. ''Why didn't you wake me when you got up?''

Chad snuck a peek at Rafe from beneath the brim of his black Stetson. ''Cuz Rafe said you were tired and you'd get up in your own good time.''

More like he didn't want to face her this morning, Lauren thought, but declined to comment.

''I've fed the goats and chickens and even mucked out a stall!'' Chad announced with more delight than the chores warranted.

Lauren grinned, slipped into the corral and approached the trio. "Mucking out stalls, huh? I guess I did get lucky by sleeping in."

"Yep, you did," Chad said solemnly, as if he took his morning tasks very seriously. "And now that my chores are done, Rafe is going to let me ride Bronwyn."

Stopping next to Rafe, Lauren rubbed the gentle chestnut along her snout. "She's certainly a beauty."

As if understanding the compliment, Bronwyn shifted closer to Lauren and nudged her in the arm, then snuffled her neck. Lauren laughed at the fond gesture, and when she glanced toward Rafe with a smile, she caught him watching her, his expression heartbreakingly vulnerable—as if he wanted to share in her enjoyment but didn't dare. As soon as their eyes met, he immediately averted his.

"Haul yourself into the saddle, pardner," Rafe ordered Chad, and waited until the boy had seated himself on the horse.

Chad sat patiently while Rafe adjusted the stirrups for his short legs, looking like a little rodeo cowboy in his hat, western shirt, jeans and cowboy boots. "Will you watch me ride, Lauren?"

The hopeful note in his voice grabbed at Lauren, reminding her why they were here on Rafe's ranch—to give this boy a week of wonderful memories to sustain him for the uncertain years ahead. "Of course, I will. I wouldn't miss this for anything."

Finished with the stirrups, Rafe plucked his hat from a hook on a nearby post, jammed the Stetson on his head and returned to Chad. Grabbing Bronwyn's reins, he led the horse into the sun toward the end of the corral, where he opened a wide gate leading to a few acres of flat, green pasture.

Lauren followed at a more leisurely pace, listening to Rafe give Chad a few last-minute rules before giving him the okay to take off with Bronwyn. Chad turned in the saddle to glance at Lauren, his expression anxious and excited at the same time.

Knowing he sought her approval, she gave him a thumbs-up sign. "Have fun, kiddo."

Rafe patted Bronwyn on the rump, gently urging her forward into the pasture. Chad took the lead from there, gradually easing the mare into a trot. As he gained confidence he progressed to a canter, then to a full-fledged gallop. Horse and rider moved smoothly across the open field.

Rafe moved next to Lauren at the fence. She wanted to keep Chad in sight at all times, though she had to shade her eyes with her hand because of the bright sunshine.

"You ought to get yourself a hat," Rafe said, his gruff tone making the suggestion sound more like an order. "You're gonna burn that soft, smooth skin of yours before the week is out."

And he would know just how soft and smooth her skin was, considering he'd caressed it the night before. Ignoring the slight kick of her pulse at how near he stood—close enough to touch her—she sent him a brilliant smile. "A little sun never hurt me before, but thank you for caring."

Her appreciative comment startled him, and she could see that he wanted to refute the fact that he cared, even about something as inconsequential as her fair skin. But to do so would make him look defensive and trivial. No doubt miffed at her deliberate twist in words, his jaw tightened and he glanced away.

Biting back a grin, she scored herself a minor victory. By the end of next week, she was determined to breach this man's resolve. As a foster care assistant, she'd managed to do just that with more foster children than she could count, and though Rafe was a grown man, his scornful attitude was the same. *Back off and keep your distance, because I don't deserve anyone's tenderness or love.* She had plenty of experience dealing with this particular defense tactic.

She followed Rafe's line of vision to Chad, who'd taken Bronwyn to the edge of the pasture where the stretch of green grass seemed to disappear over a small hill. "Will Chad be okay on his own out there?" she asked, worried that the boy might travel out of sight.

"He'll be fine," Rafe assured her, bracing his forearms on the top rung of the fence, the length of his body falling into a deceptively relaxed pose that took the pressure off his injured leg. "I've established his boundaries so he can't go far. And he's proven that he knows his way around a horse, so I'm confident he can handle Bronwyn. She's one of my most docile mares."

Silence settled between them, and Lauren struggled for a topic of discussion, something light and easy that didn't threaten this man's emotional shields. Something to establish them as friends, which they desperately needed to make living with each other for the next week bearable.

She concentrated on Chad, the one person they had in common. The boy was having a great time riding Bronwyn and showed no signs of exhaustion or boredom. He was a natural in the saddle, very fluid and exceptionally coordinated. Chad whooped in glee as he guided the mare past Lauren and Rafe at a light, smooth gallop. His elation was infectious and made Lauren so happy her chest expanded with a soul-deep contentment.

"You see that huge smile on Chad's face?" she asked in a near whisper, unwilling to shatter the wonderful moment that wove through her. "All it takes is one of those carefree smiles from one of my foster clients to make what I do feel so gratifying."

He finally looked at her, and although she had to squint into the sun blazing behind him, there was no dismissing the mild curiosity in his pewter gaze. "What you do? Meaning granting special wishes for foster children?"

"Yeah," she said, nodding. "Right now, here on your ranch, Chad doesn't have a care or worry in the world, which is exactly the purpose of Bright Beginnings. I know it's not much in the scope of what he'll have to face in the future, but this week is something that will give him some fond memories to look back on."

He turned his upper body toward her, his height and the width of his chest blocking the sun. She had the fleeting thought that those mammoth shoulders were not only appealing to look at and even nicer to cling to, they also offered her shade from the sun's glare.

His gaze fell briefly to her mouth, and her lips tingled in response to that warm, visual touch. Too easily, she recalled the thrill of his kiss, the delicious heat and fiery passion that had ignited between them. She ached to taste him again. Maybe the next time they'd go slow, let the tantalizing hunger gradually build, and he'd glide those big, callused hands along her flesh, stroke his palms over her sensitized breasts...

"Why do you do it?"

Her heart leaped into her throat at his question, asked in a husky tone of voice that inspired all kinds of wicked answers. His intense stare unnerved her. She had the oddest feeling his thoughts had taken on a sensual spin, too, and he was trying to escape them.

"Um, do what?" she responded tentatively, hoping for a little more information before she made a complete fool of herself with her answer.

There was the faintest hint of a smile in his eyes, and then it was gone, making her wish he'd allow such a playful gesture to form on his lips so she could see how breathtakingly gorgeous a simple grin made him. "Why do you go above and beyond your job to grant these children their special wishes?"

Ah, at least it was a simple, straightforward question and not one designed to throw her libido into overdrive, as this man seemed to do too darn easily. Smoothing back a stray strand of hair that fluttered along her cheek from the breeze, she glanced at Chad, remembering the inspiration behind Bright Beginnings.

"I started with Blair Foster Care Services about five years ago, and it didn't take me long to develop a special affinity for these young children whose lives have been so emotionally shattered. When they first come to Blair for an interview, they all seem so lost, so alone and very scared." Her voice softened with emotion. "Their futures are so uncertain, you know?"

He nodded, his eyes radiating profound understanding. His silent empathy made her feel as though he'd experienced a turbulent childhood and knew exactly what a lot of foster children went through. The thought made her more curious about him, but knowing how prickly he became when she asked personal questions, she thought better of pursuing the unsettling emotions in his gaze.

Lauren had grown up with every security and advantage a child could ever need or require, and because she'd been so fortunate, she wanted to extend some joy and compassion to those less privileged. She just wished her mother understood her aspirations and heart's desire. But that was a large part of the problem—her mother never took the opportunity to understand anything about her daughter's life or the time she'd devoted to the foundation she'd established. Her parents thought of Bright Beginnings as a hobby, a way to occupy her until she got married and settled down to have a family and be the proper wife of some blue blood. Lauren wanted to get married and longed for a family of her own, but she wanted those things with a man who accepted and respected Bright Beginnings as an important part of her life. So far, none of the men Maureen Richmond had hand-picked for her had filled that requirement.

Not wanting to dwell on those troubling thoughts, she kept her mind firmly planted on the current subject—why she found her work so gratifying. "Most of the kids who are taken into child protective services are removed from their homes because of neglect, abuse or abandonment, but there are other circumstances that warrant foster care for a child, such as becoming an orphan. When I meet these foster kids for the first time to interview them, I want to offer them a bit of security, so I set up this treasure chest in my office, which I keep filled with all sorts of toys and stuffed animals. The first thing I do is let them select a special toy. It's a small token gift, but it's something that will belong to them, and offer a modicum of assurance and stability in their new environment.''

She had Rafe's complete interest and marveled at how good it felt to share her beliefs and ambitions with someone who didn't scorn what she did or brush it off as insignificant.

Crossing her arms over the top part of the fence and hooking her boot on the bottom rung, she enjoyed Rafe's undivided attention and continued. ''Every once in a while, I come across a child whose situation is beyond the norm, like Chad, for instance.'' She waved a hand toward the boy who was quickly leaving his mark on her. ''He lost both of his parents, and since he has no living relatives, he'll be placed in a foster home until he is either adopted, which I've already told you is highly unlikely at his age, or he turns eighteen and is on his own. He's already been through two temporary foster homes in the six months since his parents died. He's got a long, hard road ahead of him, and I really wanted to give him a little joy in his life, which is why I decided to grant this special request of his. And when I see how happy it's made him, even if it's just for a week, it makes what I do worthwhile.''

Rafe tipped his hat back, regarding her speculatively. ''I have to say, what you do is incredibly selfless, but *how* do you do it? I mean, doesn't it get expensive granting all these wishes?''

Her shoulders lifted in a small shrug. ''I can afford it,'' she assured him with a smile. ''Bright

Beginnings was set up with a substantial trust fund that was endowed to me by my grandmother two years ago, when I turned twenty-five. I'm an only child, and I was her only grandchild, so she was quite generous. I'm putting the money toward a good cause, and I'd like to think that if she were still alive, she'd approve of what I do." Unlike her mother, who felt she was being frivolous. Despite her mother's objections, Lauren didn't regret her decision. The foundation brought her as much pleasure as working with the children.

She exhaled on a long sigh, which the breeze carried away. "One day, I hope to do more for these underprivileged kids."

He cocked his head inquisitively, looking handsome and very likable. "Like what?"

"Something on a grander scale, possibly, like a camp, or even purchase land for horseback riding adventures," she said, excitement infusing her voice. "Something fun that would give these foster kids a start in the right direction."

He digested that, but there was a more prying light in his gaze. "You come from money, then?"

There was no censure in his deep voice, just a mild hunch he openly expressed. "My parents are wealthy, yes, but I like to think I've made it on my own, without their financial support. I earn my own paycheck, I financed my own car, and I pay my own rent in an apartment I share with my roommate, Amy. Everything I own I've bought with money I've earned."

Begrudging respect flitted across his face. "And your parents, what do they do?"

"My father is a criminal lawyer with his own firm,

and my mother works real hard at trying to find me a suitable husband.'' She'd used a humorous tone of voice, but the burden of her mother's interference in her love life was no joke.

Rafe blinked lazily, and as if seeing past her attempt at levity, asked, "Don't you want to get married?"

"Oh, absolutely," she said without a moment's hesitation. "But with a man of my own choosing."

His smoky gaze flickered down the length of her, taking a slow, leisurely journey that kindled little brushfires of awareness beneath her skin and tightened the tips of her breasts. By the time his eyes returned to hers, her heart beat in an unsteady rhythm.

"I would think you'd have hordes of suitors to pick from," he murmured, his tone velvet-smooth and very distracting.

Struggling not to let Rafe know how strongly he affected her with just a look and that rough-and-sexy voice of his, she turned her attention to Chad. The boy had dismounted and was plucking wildflowers from a patch of bright, colorful blooms blowing in the breeze. A small, pleased smile touched the corner of her mouth, and she experienced relief that the foster care system hadn't jaded Chad's sensitive, giving nature...yet. The years ahead would take their toll, she knew.

"I've dated," she admitted to Rafe, guessing by the stall in conversation that he expected an answer. "But I'm holding out for something no one has sparked yet."

"And what's that?" he drawled.

She took a deep breath and admitted, "Love."

A mocking light entered his storm-gray eyes. "You believe in fairy tales, huh?"

Irritation bristled up her spine. "Is it so wrong to believe that love exists and to hold out for it?" Her question was direct, and certainly a challenge for this cynical man who believed he didn't need anyone.

"No, I suppose not," he admitted gruffly, not looking at her.

"I guess I want that fairy tale so badly because I don't want the kind of relationship my parents have," she explained softly.

That confession surprised him, and he turned his head. His confusion was evident. "Which is?"

That same old sadness tugged at her when she thought of her parents' situation. She was determined not to repeat their mistake. "A marriage of convenience."

He lifted a dark brow, unable to conceal the intrigue that leaped into his gaze.

She explained. "They got married because my mother was pregnant with me, and though they're still together, they live separate lives. I want a marriage based on respect and common interest. Is it so wrong to want love and a man who respects what I do?"

"No," he said quietly, and with more kindness and compassion than he'd shown her thus far. "No, there's nothing wrong with that at all."

She dragged her fingers through her hair, feeling a twinge of frustration over her mother's meddling. She thought of her ideal husband, whom she'd yet to encounter. "The combination hasn't been an easy one to find, especially when my mother keeps foisting these pompous, arrogant men on me, who all want a trophy wife and trained hostess more than an equal partner in marriage.'' She shuddered to lighten the moment, and saw his mouth twitch. When he realized what almost happened, he scrubbed a hand along his jaw, wiping away the amused expression that nearly dared to grace his face.

Vast disappointment coursed through Lauren. At the moment, she would have offered her entire trust account to see those full lips of his curve into a warm, engaging smile. Or to hear a rich, deep chuckle rumble from his chest. She knew he had it in him—under lock and key, no doubt.

Grouchy, grumpy, gorgeous cowboy!

"So, what about you, Rafe?" she asked, eyeing him casually, more than ready to put a few wrinkles in that staid composure of his. "You ever been married?"

Rafe's entire body tensed at her personal query, and he fought in vain to maintain a bland expression. "Nope."

"Close to it, maybe?" she wheedled.

Damn, the woman was nosy, and pushy. "Nope. Never." He'd had a few relationships over the years while traveling the circuit, but none of them had developed beyond a flirtatious fling. And after the accident, well, there wasn't a woman around who deserved to be saddled with an S.O.B. like himself. He knew that, accepted it and lived with it.

She frowned at him, her bluer-than-the-sky-above eyes twinkling with too much mischief. "Don't you want a wife and a passel of kids to fill up this big ranch of yours?"

Inadequacies and fears swamped him, making that particular wish an impossibility. "Nope."

"Aw, come on," she said, gently nudging his arm with hers, the brush of her skin against his electrifying his nerves. "I find that hard to believe. Doesn't it ever get lonely living out here all by yourself?"

All the time. His belly clenched at the unexpected realization. "I like the way my life is," he said, wondering if he was trying to convince her or himself.

"Isolated and alone?" she offered impudently.

Anger flashed through him. "Uncomplicated and simplified."

His abrupt manner didn't faze her. Instead, she leaned close and grinned at him. "Ah, and here I thought you were a risk taker."

Trying not to think about how near she stood, how good she smelled or the soft, unconscious press of her breast against his arm, he moved his mouth into a tight line. "I stopped taking risks a year ago when my career ended."

"Now you play it safe, hm?" she reflected, backing off just enough to give him some breathing room that didn't include her light, feminine fragrance. "By keeping yourself secluded out here on your ranch and trying to be unsociable? If no one gets too close, then you won't have to risk that heart of yours, huh?"

He narrowed his gaze, but she wasn't at all intimidated by the menacing look he summoned. "Anybody ever tell you that you've got a sassy mouth that's gonna get you into trouble?"

She blushed but didn't retreat. "You're the first, and just so you don't worry overly much about it, I can handle trouble, cowboy."

He didn't refute her claim. She'd established her capability of handling trouble last night in the kitchen, when she'd taken his brand of orneriness and returned it in spades. The thing was, he wanted to give this feisty, stubborn woman more trouble of the sensual variety. That kiss they'd shared had kept him aroused all night long and still swirled in his belly like hundred-proof whiskey. Images of making love to her, of how soft and giving her body would be beneath his, burned in his mind.

Wanting her was dangerous and incredibly stupid, yet knowing that didn't make a lick of difference to his unruly hormones. The craving to taste her again clouded all reason. The warm awareness he detected in her eyes wrapped around him, coaxing and irresistible. His heart thundered against his ribs, and he lowered his head toward hers a fraction. Her chin tilted up in an effort to meet him halfway, and her damp lips parted in anticipation, releasing a soft sigh.

The sound of a horse galloping their way broke the spell between them. Rafe jerked and swore beneath his breath, grateful at the timely interruption and furious at himself for being so careless. What was he thinking to kiss her again?

The disappointment etching Lauren's features faded into a smile as Chad brought Bronwyn to a stop in front of the fence where they stood. Oblivious to the sensual undercurrents between adults, he thrust out his bouquet toward Lauren.

"I picked these for you," he said, looking uncertain and hopeful at the same time.

She took the flowers he offered, her eyes shining with adoration for the young boy and his thoughtfulness. Lifting the flowers to her nose, she inhaled their light, floral fragrance. "Thank you, Chad. These are lovely."

Chad beamed.

"You getting hungry for a sandwich, kiddo?" she asked.

"A little," he admitted. "But can I ride Bronwyn for just a little while longer?"

The pleading note in Chad's voice got the best of Rafe. "Ten more minutes," he said, ignoring the knowing smile Lauren cast his way. "Then we need to cool her down."

"Yippee!" Chad cheered, then took off with Bronwyn for another trip around the pasture.

"So, do you ride?" Rafe asked Lauren in an attempt to make conversation once they were alone again.

"I've had a lesson or two," she said, her quirky smile and lilting voice telling him she was being modest about her ability to ride a horse.

"My sister invited us to her place for a barbecue tomorrow. I was thinking we could ride over since she lives on the property that adjoins mine."

"I'd love that."

He discovered he was looking forward to the outing, too. Before he realized what he was doing, his finger touched her nose and traced a path across the color blossoming along her soft cheeks. The gesture surprised them both, and he quickly lowered his hand and cleared his throat. "Your, ah, nose is getting pink, and so are your cheeks. I'll pick you up a hat the next time I'm in town."

She ducked her head shyly, a quality he found fascinating in such a strong-willed woman.

"I think I'll go start lunch," she said, backing away.

She walked toward the gate to exit the corral, but turned before she got there. She held those precious, already wilting flowers against her chest, looking like a wholesome country girl, making something deep inside him unfurl and ache.

Her sass returned, kicking up the tips of her mouth in an impish grin and shimmering in her dark blue eyes. "Oh, and Rafe, you're not half bad when you're being sociable. Better be careful, or some woman might take all that congeniality too seriously and get the notion that you need yourself a wife."

He tried to summon a scowl at her subtle mockery and found himself shaking his head instead, hard-pressed to hold back the grin twitching the corners of his lips.

CHAPTER FIVE

"So, TELL me, has my brother been on his best behavior?"

Lauren smiled at Rafe's sister, Kristin, detecting the humor in her voice and in her green eyes. They'd arrived at Kristin and James's a half hour earlier on horseback, and after a round of introductions and idle chitchat, the two broad-shouldered men and Chad had taken off toward a corral stabling a new foal with Blackie, James's border collie, running and playing at Chad's heels.

Lauren didn't mind the males heading off on their own. In fact, she welcomed the reprieve, especially from her host. Oh, she and Rafe had settled into an amicable truce since their discussion yesterday, but this moody man with all his deep, dark secrets consumed too much of her thoughts and made her pulse race with that sexy, rugged masculine appeal of his. She wasn't one to indulge in impulsive, frivolous attractions, no matter how gorgeous the man, yet Rafe made her want to throw caution to the Wyoming breeze and give in to the intense awareness they both seemed to be fighting.

To do so would only send her back to California with a wealth of heartache. Her time with Rafe was temporary with no room for intimate complications, and he wasn't the type to accept a woman into the solitary life he'd created for himself. A brief fling was out of the question for her. She was holding out for love.

Sitting across from Kristin at the redwood picnic table situated under a large shade tree in the yard, she firmly rerouted her thoughts to the woman's question. "Considering Chad and I are disrupting his life for a week, yes, Rafe's been pretty hospitable."

"Chad is a wonderful little boy, and I don't think it would hurt for Rafe to have some disruption in his life." Kristin reached for the covered pitcher of iced tea on the table and poured them each a plastic tumbler full of the cool drink. "This is good for him. The past year has been difficult, with his accident and all. I'm really hoping that you and Chad make him realize what a recluse he's been and that he's only hurting himself. Nothing I say seems to make a difference."

Lauren wasn't having much luck in that department, either. She agreed that Rafe was hurting way deep inside, yet she didn't know enough about Rafe's past to make assumptions about the cynical man. She toyed with the idea of asking Kristin what happened to make Rafe so hard and bitter but thought better of it. If she ever learned the truth, she wanted to hear it from Rafe.

Taking a drink of her iced tea, Lauren followed Kristin's gaze to where Rafe, James and Chad were doting on the new foal. James was talking to Chad, and the boy laughed at something he said. A wistful smile curved Kristin's mouth, mingling with the pure love that etched her features.

"So, how did you and James meet?" Lauren asked curiously, puzzled by the emotions she witnessed. "He's a wonderful man and seems crazy about you.'' Their devotion for one another had been immediately evident to Lauren in the way the couple looked at one another and the gentle, reverent way James touched his wife. If Rafe doubted love existed, he only needed to take a closer look at his sister and brother-in-law to affirm its existence.

Kristin blushed a becoming shade of pink. ''I've known James all my life, actually. His family grew up in Cedar Creek, and I went to school with him, but we were always just friends. It wasn't until after my father died, about seven years ago, that we really noticed one another. Rafe hired James as a foreman to keep up the spread while he was off traveling the circuit and, well, one thing led to another, and we fell in love.''

''So this is your family's ranch, then?''

''Yes.'' Kristin unwrapped a plate of lemon cake and urged Lauren to take a slice, which she did. ''After James and I married, Rafe took a parcel of the land and built his own place, and James started up a cattle operation, which has done quite well.''

Looking around, Lauren had to agree. The land was fertile, the barn and stables in good shape, the livestock well cared for. The house Rafe and Kristin had grown up in appeared to be newly renovated, inside and out. The charming old Victorian, built of weathered white clapboard, had an appealing wrap-around porch complete with a hanging swing. The yard was manicured and huge. The only thing missing from Kristin and James's loving marriage and comfortable life was children.

''Do you and James plan to have kids?'' she asked, licking the stickiness from the delicious cake off her fingers.

A pained looked crossed Kristin's face, which Lauren immediately caught.

"I'm sorry," she apologized, unsure what painful memories she'd tapped into. She didn't want Kristin to feel obligated to unearth them. "I didn't mean to pry—"

"No, it's quite all right." Kristin took a deep breath, as if to gather her composure, and smiled, but the smile didn't reach her eyes. "James and I would love a family, but I'm not able to have children."

Lauren felt as though she'd been slammed in her stomach with a fist. She couldn't imagine the emotional anguish of being unable to conceive a baby. Her heart went out to Kristin. "I'm so sorry to hear that."

"I still find it hard to believe myself," she said sadly as she ran a finger down the condensation forming on her tumbler. "A few months after James and I married, I was diagnosed with endometriosis and had to have a hysterectomy. James has been great about the fact that we'll never have kids, but I think about it all the time. I try to console myself with the second-graders I teach during the school year, but it's times like this, during the summer, when I don't have that daily contact with kids, that I feel the loss more acutely."

Lauren nodded, her feminine side comprehending that pain. "Have you ever thought about adoption?"

Kristin lifted a shoulder in a shrug. "It's crossed my mind, but I'm just not sure about it."

"Maybe you should think about it seriously," Lauren suggested, and took a drink of her iced tea. "There are so many children out there like Chad who need a loving home, unless you'd prefer to adopt a baby instead of a grown child.''

"I don't know," Kristin admitted, a soft smile of longing touching her mouth. "There's just something so sweet and innocent about a little baby."

"I understand." And Lauren truly did. Most couples who made the choice to adopt wanted a newborn, an uninfluenced infant wholly dependent on no one but them.

A squeal of laughter made them both look onto the lawn, where James was tossing a Frisbee to Chad, who then sailed the disc to Blackie. The agile dog jumped into the air, caught the Frisbee in his mouth and trotted with it to James to begin the cycle again. Rafe stood underneath a nearby tree, his back braced against the thick trunk, his right knee angled to take the pressure off his leg. The brim of his hat covered his eyes, but Lauren felt him watching her, as she had many times since yesterday. That reserve of his was frustrating and maddening.

Smile for me, Rafe. Just once. Come on, it'll feel so good you might not want to stop.

Her mental telepathy didn't reach him, or he ignored the vibes. Stubborn man that he was, she suspected the latter.

"I think what you do for those foster kids is incredibly generous," Kristin said, reining in Lauren's wandering thoughts.

She glanced at Rafe's sister. "I enjoy making them happy."

"Rafe told me a little about Chad's situation. Losing both parents must have been incredibly difficult for him."

Lauren agreed, knowing that Chad still struggled with the loss of the only family he'd ever known.

"What will happen to Chad after this week when you return to California?"

"He'll be placed in another foster home. I'm really hoping to find him a family that he fits in with. It's not always easy to do."

Kristin's eyes rounded in surprise, and her gaze drifted to the young boy who seemed so carefree and playful with Blackie and James. "I can't imagine him not fitting in. He's a good boy, has a good disposition, and he's so very warm and bright."

"Human nature being what it is, personalities don't always click," Lauren said, having seen the harsher side of foster care. "Sometimes it takes a few foster homes before we find the right family for a client."

Kristin digested that, her expression filled with compassion. "I hope he finds a family that will give him all the love and attention he deserves."

Lauren smiled. "Yeah, me, too."

Three hours later, after eating barbecued hamburgers, homemade potato salad and a fresh fruit medley, everyone converged indoors to relax and let their meal settle. Chad excitedly announced that he'd brought his scrapbook of Rafe and his rodeo days, and withdrew the album from the backpack he'd worn on the ride over.

The canvas bag held all Chad's most treasured possessions—a few photos of his parents, his scrapbook of Rafe's career, a worn and tattered floppy-eared bunny he'd had since infancy and a couple of his favorite action figures. Lauren knew the backpack was a security blanket for Chad. He rarely went far without it.

"Here's a picture of Rafe when he won the championship for the third time in a row," Chad said to Kristin and James, who sat on either side of him on the sofa. All three looked at the color photograph taken from a trade magazine.

Situated on the love seat across from the sofa, with Rafe sitting beside her, Lauren was able to fully enjoy the way Chad effortlessly charmed Kristin and James with his animated conversation and his infectious enthusiasm. The boy had a captive audience and took advantage of their undivided attention. Lauren noticed a special connection between the boy and James, a natural paternal rapport that went beyond the politeness of being warm and amicable to an orphaned boy.

"And here's an article on Rafe when he rode Twister for the full eight seconds and won the purse for that event at the Wild, Wild West Rodeo. Lucky number seventeen!" Chad drawled like a seasoned rodeo announcer, making everyone but Rafe laugh. Chad glanced across the room to the man he idolized, his gaze expectant. "Do you remember that win, Rafe?"

"Sure do," Rafe replied, his low, even tone disguising just how uncomfortable this trip down memory lane seemed to make him.

Chad continued, pointing to pictures, features and write-ups on Rafe he'd collected over the years. The more Chad acclaimed Rafe and his prestigious career, the more Lauren detected a growing change in the man sitting beside her. The tension radiating off him was nearly palpable, and she resisted the strong urge to lay her fingers over the hand absently rubbing his right thigh in a restless motion. A small consolation, considering how troubled and anxious this entire scenario made him.

"This is my favorite article," Chad announced, awe in his voice. He read the headline. "From PRCA Champion to Hero. It's All in a Day's Work." Chad's gaze met Rafe's, the emotion in the boy's eyes heartfelt. "I know you can't ride bulls anymore, but saving that other man's life was very brave of you."

Rafe abruptly stood, his expression one of a cornered animal. He picked up his Stetson from the coffee table next to the couch, jammed it on his head and gave the occupants of the room a curt nod. "I think I'll go saddle up the horses so we can head back home before nightfall."

A combination of confusion and hurt knit Chad's brow, and he chewed on his lower lip as he watched the man he held in such high esteem leave the living room.

Kristin's gaze met Lauren's. Kristin silently urged her to follow Rafe and somehow make amends. Lauren felt inadequately equipped to handle Rafe's emotional demons, but neither did she want to add to Chad's disappointment.

"I'll go help Rafe with the horses," she said.

Kristin nodded. "How about you help me with dessert, Chad?" she asked, ruffling his hair to divert his attention. "I made a fresh apple pie this morning, and I can warm you up a slice."

"With a scoop of vanilla ice cream on top," James suggested with a grin and bobbing eyebrows as he placed an affectionate hand on Chad's shoulder to guide him toward the kitchen. "That's the *only* way to enjoy apple pie."

"Can I have two scoops of ice cream?" he asked guilelessly, prompting the adults to laugh.

Knowing the young boy was sufficiently occupied, Lauren took a deep, fortifying breath and went in search of her reluctant hero.

"You need to work on your manners, Dalton. Your departure back there was a little rude."

Rafe stiffened at the sound of Lauren's mocking voice, but he didn't turn to acknowledge her as he slipped a bit into Bronwyn's mouth. "What do you want, Lauren?" he asked gruffly, unsettled by what had transpired at the house and the multitude of feelings Chad's innocent words had unleashed.

She entered the corral and stopped in front of Bronwyn, who greeted her with a gentle nuzzling against her jaw, making Lauren smile and croon sweet words to the mare. To Rafe, she said, "I thought you might need some help."

He suspected her motives for seeking him out were more self-serving than that. "I have a problem with my leg, not my arms and hands."

"You also seem to have a problem admitting you're a hero for saving that bull rider's life," she replied impudently.

Adjusting the straps of the headpiece over Bronwyn's ears, he fought to hold onto his escalating temper. "I can't admit to something I'm not." He pinned Lauren with a dark look that warned her to quit probing. "Chad is hanging on to an illusion created by the press."

"Is it so wrong for a child to believe in heroes?" she asked softly.

Just like she believed in love and happily ever after. "Not where they don't exist." He looped Bronwyn's reins loosely over a rail, stalked around Lauren and headed into the stable to retrieve the rest of their gear.

He heard her quick footsteps behind him, then her hand curled around his arm, bringing him to a stop.

Determination lined her features. "Quit brushing this subject off as inconsequential, Rafe."

He glared, perfecting the scowl that kept most people at bay.

She crossed her arms and waited. "I'm not letting this go until you explain what happened at the house a few minutes ago. Since the day I first met you you've dodged this hero issue, acting as though it's an insult to your character. The people in town put up with your uncivilized behavior because they don't want to confront you. Well, I'm tired of dealing with your moods and your cynicism, and you know why?"

He didn't answer, though he had a feeling she was going to give him her opinion on the matter whether he wanted it or not.

"Because I know this gruff, don't-get-close-to-me attitude is all a facade to hide something deeper and more painful," she said.

He propped his fists on his hips and shifted his weight to his left leg. "And how would you know that?" he challenged in a derisive drawl.

Her perfect, kissable mouth pursed. "People who have been hurt tend to blame themselves for things that aren't necessarily their fault. I see that in my line of work all the time. Guilt is a powerful emotion.'' When he said nothing, her eyes flashed with irritation. "Dammit, Rafe, what happened to make you such a cynical man?"

Instincts he'd honed the past year urged him to ignore her question and walk away, but the need to unburden himself was undeniable. The pain twisting inside him was near unbearable. So was the awful realization that he'd inherited traits from his father that he wasn't proud of.

Wearily, he sat on a bench braced against the nearby wall and scrubbed a hand along his jaw. "I don't deserve Chad's praise, or anyone else's, for what I did for Keith," he told her, his voice low and as honest as he'd ever been. "I feel like a fraud for letting Chad believe I'm a hero."

"Why?" She shook her head in puzzlement, her silky hair brushing her shoulders with the movement. "You saved that rider and risked your own life in the process. You took the brunt of that bull's anger while rescuing Keith, which ended your career. If that isn't heroic, I don't know what is."

He rubbed his palm over the scar on his thigh through his jeans while old, bitter emotions rose to the surface, nearly choking him with guilt. "How do you think Chad would feel about me being a hero if he knew I was the reason Keith nearly got killed?"

Lauren's blue eyes widened, and she pressed her back against the stall door behind her as she absorbed his confession. After a moment, she said, "I find it hard to believe that you could be responsible for a bull throwing a rider. That's the nature of the sport."

"Normally, it is, but I pushed Keith to get on that bull before he was ready." Rafe stood and paced in front of her, caught up in his personal grief. "The kid was scared spitless and in no way prepared for the power and force of Cyclone's fury. I *knew* that, yet I convinced him to get on that bull and ride him like a man."

"Ultimately, it was Keith's choice to ride Cyclone," Lauren argued vehemently. "You're not the black-hearted guy you want everyone to believe, Rafe."

He stopped in front of her, unable to understand how this woman who didn't know him at all refused to believe the worst about him, even after he'd given her all the contemptible facts. Unable to understand, too, how much he ached to accept her faith and unconditional gentleness.

The awareness that inevitably swirled between them began its slow, sensual pull on his senses. His heart hammered in his chest as he gazed into her eyes, the depths as clear and breathtaking as the vast Wyoming sky. It was dim and cool in the stable. Their surroundings were made more intimate by the quickening of her breathing. The provocative sound elicited a very male response from him.

Unable to resist her allure, he caressed her soft cheek with the back of his knuckles, the silky texture of her skin a direct, arousing contrast to his rough, callused hands. "You're the kind of woman who believes the best in everyone, aren't you?" Surprisingly, his tone was devoid of the criticism he'd used to keep his distance from this woman, and instead held reluctant resignation.

She shivered delicately when he brushed the tips of his fingers along her neck and touched the sensitive spot behind her ear. "Everyone deserves that chance.'' Her voice was husky with desire, rich with a growing need.

''Not me,'' he refuted in a raspy murmur, still unable to shake the convictions he'd clung to for too long.

A soft, feminine smile curved her mouth. ''Especially you, Rafe.'' Lifting a hand, she pressed her palm against his chest, not to push him away, but to urge him closer to the heat and hunger building between them. ''What happened was a tragic mistake, but you're a good person, and I don't believe you'd intentionally hurt anyone.''

After a year of living in the dark world he'd created for himself, after tormenting his conscience with guilt and recriminations, her compassion warmed his bruised and battered soul. She tangled up his emotions, made him long for things he had no right wanting. And regardless of every solid reason he had for avoiding her brand of tenderness, he was powerless to stop the fierce need she evoked. There was something about her that pulled at him, made him want to expose his darkest secrets, his most vulnerable fears.

He stared at her generous mouth, remembering too well how openly and honestly she responded to him—no pretenses, just pure pleasure and a deep, vital craving like nothing he'd ever experienced. He wanted to taste her again, appease the addiction he seemed to have for her.

She watched him with those perceptive eyes veiled by long lashes, waiting patiently for him to make up his mind, her hand warm and still over his frantically beating heart. When he finally gave in to temptation and slowly lowered his head to claim her mouth, she didn't resist him. She brazenly met him halfway, her lips parted and damp and ready.

Their first kiss had been heated and angry and filled with reckless thoroughness. This one was a slow, drugging discovery. He gradually eased her into a deeper embrace, seducing her with the warm slide of his lips, the tantalizing glide of his tongue against hers. What the first kiss lacked in subtlety, this one more than made up for in finesse.

He lifted his hands and framed her face between his palms. He stepped closer, imprinting his body with her supple curves, inflaming his senses with erotic, forbidden thoughts that fueled the fantasies he had of her naked and eager beneath him. Her soft breasts were crushed against his chest, and she arched to get closer still, then moaned in frustration when the contact didn't seem to satisfy her.

The flare of anticipation between them was too much and not enough. Overwhelming emotions gripped him—the tenderness he'd sworn he didn't have within him and the raw desire he'd fought to suppress since the moment this sassy, stubborn lady had breezed into his life and turned it upside down. He poured everything into that intimate kiss, knowing too soon she'd be gone and his world would return to the lonely, solitary existence he'd created for himself. If memories were the only thing he had to keep him company during the cold, long winter, then he planned to store up plenty.

He cupped her breast through her shirt, relishing the way her soft, feminine flesh swelled against his palm. He grazed his thumb over the tip until it hardened beneath his touch. She gasped, breaking their kiss, and he found himself looking into her bright blue eyes, falling deeper into the spell she seemed to cast over him.

"Rafe," she whispered achingly.

The one word held a wealth of possibilities, and he struggled to maintain some semblance of control over the situation. "We can't do this," he said, even as his hands skimmed her sides, putting to memory her lush curves.

"I...I can't help wanting you, Rafe."

Her honesty humbled him. Nuzzling the curve of her neck, he breathed deeply of her scent. "It's just a bad case of lust," he said, knowing his words were a lie. A one-time tumble wouldn't be enough to get this woman out of his system. Lifting his head, he smoothed her hair from her face. "Our lives are too different for it to be anything more than that, Lauren. You've got your work in California, and I'm not looking for anything long-term or serious."

She nodded, but that didn't erase the more troubling emotions in her eyes. "So what are we going to do about this attraction between us?"

"Nothing." The word rang with finality, but didn't stop him from dipping his head and stealing another kiss, and yet another. "Nothing at all," he muttered against her lips.

Before he broke his own rule and changed his mind about making love to her, he moved away, reminding himself of the many complications of getting involved with a citified woman like Lauren. Not only did they live in different worlds, but she was looking for love, which wasn't on his agenda. Mix that with her mother, who had her own itinerary of finding a suitable man for her daughter, and they were courting disaster.

He blew out a long breath to release the sexual tension coiling in his belly, and lower, and worked real hard at softening his expression. "Come on," he said, nodding toward the tack room. "You said you came down here to help me with the horses, and I plan to put you to work."

CHAPTER SIX

LAUREN walked into the kitchen early the following morning and found Rafe staring out the window over the sink, drinking a cup of coffee, looking relaxed but lost in thought.

She could relate to the preoccupation. The kiss they'd shared the evening before was still fresh in her mind, as was the conversation they'd had about his accident and the responsibility he felt over Keith's injury. She understood part of where his guilt stemmed from. But she sensed there was something deeper and more personal at the root of Rafe's emotional angst.

Knowing it would do no good to pressure him for something he wasn't ready to talk about, she concentrated on strengthening the friendship they were gradually forging.

She stepped into the kitchen and greeted him in a bright and cheery tone of voice. "Good morning."

He turned around, his gaze taking in her casual summer dress and sandals before returning to her face. Pleasure and something more vibrant flitted across his expression, making her pulse pick up its tempo.

"Morning." His drawl was warm, friendly and devoid of the underlying gruffness that had once colored his tone.

She'd definitely made progress with Rafe's attitude, though her ultimate goal was to see a smile on

95

those sexy lips of his. She was confident of prodding one from him before the end of the week. The man didn't stand a chance against her efforts. Granted, he wasn't easily swayed by a toy, like the young foster children she dealt with, but she planned to barrage him with humor and laughter and her own smiles until he had no choice but to respond in kind.

Keeping her satisfied grin under wraps, she headed toward the coffeepot on the counter. She took a mug from the cupboard, filled it with the steaming brew, then added cream and sugar.

She could feel Rafe watching her, and her skin flushed with a shimmering warmth. The strain of the past few days had eased between them after their confrontation at Kristin's the evening before, but now a new kind of tension had taken its place—a sensual awareness teeming with anticipation.

Lauren leaned a hip against the counter, and took a sip of her coffee. "I was thinking of taking Chad to Fran's for breakfast for those banana pecan pancakes she'd offered. Will you come with us?"

He suddenly shifted. "You two go ahead," he said, dumping the last of his coffee into the sink. "I've got things I need to get done around here."

He wasn't a very good liar, but she didn't call him on his excuse. She suspected he didn't want to venture into town with her and Chad in tow and deal with the speculation that would no doubt circulate, but she wasn't going to let him off that easily. "Can't they wait an hour or two?" she cajoled in her sweetest voice. "I'd really like for you to come along, and I know Chad would enjoy you being there, too."

He hesitated, his mouth thinning in indecision as he wavered.

She produced her most persuasive expression. "Please?"

"All right," he said after another long moment passed, and gave his head a slight shake, as if he couldn't believe he was giving in to her whims. "I need to pick up a few things at Gentry's feed store anyway."

She didn't believe that excuse, either, but considering she'd gotten exactly what she'd wanted, she wasn't about to argue his reasons for accepting the invitation.

A half hour later, the three of them entered Fran's Diner. Lauren was determined to improve Rafe's reputation with the townsfolk. Surprisingly, and without her prompting, Rafe nodded politely to the patrons he knew as they walked to a vacant table in the middle of the restaurant. In the process he seemed to salvage a small portion of the respect he'd lost the past year. Reclaiming his social status in Cedar Creek would be a slow, gradual process, Lauren knew, but Rafe's new attitude was an excellent start in that direction—as long as he kept up his sociable disposition after she and Chad returned to California.

Andrea waited on them again, though the sparks that had crackled between her and Rafe had ebbed to a mutual courtesy. She took their orders and promised Chad a stack of the best banana pecan pancakes he'd ever tasted.

A few minutes later, the only other waitress in the establishment came up to their table and filled their cups with fresh, hot coffee. "Hi, Rafe," she said, a pleasant smile lighting up her young, pretty face.

"Hello, Sally," he replied just as cordially, but without the smile, then went on to introduce the other woman to Lauren. "Sally, this is Lauren Richmond. Lauren, Sally Morris, my sister's best friend."

Lauren shook the woman's slim hand. "It's very nice to meet you."

"Same here," Sally said, genuinely warm and sweet. "I've heard so much about you and Chad, mainly from Kristin. It seems Chad has become a little celebrity in Cedar Creek. There isn't anyone in this town that hasn't heard of you, and him, and the foundation you represent. We all think what you do is pretty special."

"It's a labor of love," Lauren admitted, casting a fond look at Chad.

"My son, Randy, is here for breakfast, too, and he's sitting up at the counter." Sally motioned toward a young, dark-haired boy looking expectantly their way. "He was wondering if Chad could sit with him and they could eat their breakfast together."

Chad's hopeful gaze flickered from the boy who'd extended the kind invitation to Lauren. "Can I?"

Seeing no harm in Chad making a new friend, and knowing she'd be within seeing and hearing distance, she granted Chad permission. "Go ahead."

Chad scrambled from the booth and sat on the stool next to Randy. Before long, the two boys were talking and laughing and getting along wonderfully, Lauren and Rafe forgotten in Chad's excitement at finding a companion his own age.

Lauren glanced at Rafe. "I guess you being a rodeo star is starting to wear off with Chad," she commented with amusement. "You're becoming a regular old guy who used to ride bulls."

Rafe curled his long fingers around his coffee mug, humor glimmering briefly in his pewter gaze. "That's exactly what I am—just a simple man who raises Quarter Horses."

Hardly simple, Lauren mused as she regarded Rafe from across the table. Complex and moody were more apt descriptions, but she wasn't about the spoil the affable moment by telling him so.

Light, easy conversation accompanied their breakfast, and even though Lauren knew Rafe would never admit it, she suspected he enjoyed their relaxed, nonthreatening verbal exchange, which centered around his Quarter Horse operation.

When their meal ended, he reached for the check Andrea placed on the edge of the table. Lauren's fingers shot out to beat him to the bill and landed on the back of his hand, flattening his palm to the table with the stub trapped beneath.

"Breakfast is on me," she said, ignoring the warmth of his skin, the intimacy of the situation and the fluttering in her belly.

His sensual gaze met hers, masculine awareness swirling with something more determined in the depths of his eyes. "That might be the way you do it in California, but letting a woman pay for my breakfast wouldn't reflect too well on my manners here in Cedar Creek."

She rolled her eyes dramatically. "Since when have you been concerned about public appearances or manners?"

His thumb stroked hers, a subtle caress that caused her pulse to quicken. "Since this morning," he murmured, the low words reaching her ears only.

She stared at him, the world around them receding

as she absorbed the impact of his simple statement, which held a very significant message. He was willing to try to make amends for his behavior and attitude since meeting her, and he was starting here and now. She was so overwhelmed and delighted by this subtle transformation in Rafe, she didn't notice anyone approaching their table until someone cleared their throat to get their attention.

"Uh, excuse me," a male voice said, the tone indicating discomfort in intruding on what no doubt looked like a shared private moment between her and Rafe.

Realizing just how affectionate their situation appeared to the patrons of Fran's, Lauren jerked her hand back, which only made their innocent hand-holding look even more controversial. She glanced at the man standing beside their table and recognized him as the editor who'd come to Rafe's ranch the day she'd arrived with Chad.

An automatic smile formed on her lips. "Hi, it's Jason, isn't it?"

"Yes, ma'am," he replied courteously, his gaze moving from Rafe to her. "Am I intruding on something personal here?"

Lauren had the fleeting thought that Rafe wasn't the only one who'd developed some decorum in dealing with people. The belligerent editor who'd been so confrontational the first time she'd met him had brushed up on his professional skills, and as a result came across as approachable—likable, even.

"No, you're not intruding on anything at all," Lauren replied pleasantly. "Rafe and I were just debating cultural differences."

Rafe's lips twitched mischievously, sharing the private joke.

Puzzlement creased Jason's brows, but Lauren didn't expect him to understand her deliberately cryptic comment. "What can I do for you, Jason?" she prompted.

He pushed his hands into the front pockets of his trousers, his expression subdued. "I was wondering if I might be able to ask you a few questions about your foundation. I'd really like to write an article for the Cedar Creek *Gazette*, with your permission, of course."

"Absolutely," she agreed, and scooted over on the vinyl bench seat for Jason to sit next to her. Rafe said nothing. It was apparent in the first five minutes that the editor had decided to take a conservative approach. He kept his line of questioning focused on Bright Beginnings, on the foundation's purpose, on Lauren's future goals. He got enough information about her and Chad to fill a two-page spread in Friday's edition of the *Gazette*. All the while, Rafe sat on the other side of the table and listened quietly to their discussion.

At the end of the interview, Jason finally acknowledged Rafe. "I want to apologize for the way I handled things the other day at your place." His voice was gruff, but sincere.

"Likewise," Rafe offered in apology.

Jason folded his notepad, set it on the table and placed his pencil on top. "Would you mind if I asked you a question, Rafe, off the record?"

He gave a one-shouldered shrug that was reserved and cautious. "All right."

"What made you grant Chad's wish?"

"My reason for originally agreeing to Chad's request has changed over the past couple of days," he said with quiet honesty. "At first, I did it for personal reasons I'd rather not discuss. Now that I've met Chad, I'm doing it because the boy deserves the chance at the best possible future he can make for himself, and it all starts here, with him believing in wishes and dreams and the impossible."

At Rafe's profound revelation, Lauren's throat tightened with a rush of emotion. His statement echoed the reason Bright Beginnings was such a large part of her life. His incentive for granting Chad's request paralleled her beliefs. She realized how special and compassionate Rafe truly was, despite his surly facade.

Jason accepted Rafe's answer with a glint of respect in his eyes. Done with his interview, he stood and shook first Rafe's hand, then hers, his touch lingering longer than necessary. "Enjoy the rest of your stay in Cedar Creek, Lauren."

Smiling, she pulled her hand from his warm grasp, and he let it go. "I will, thank you."

He walked away from their table, but after a few steps turned, his expression boyishly charming. "Say, since you're not leaving until Sunday, would you happen to be free Friday evening?"

Lauren opened her mouth to reply, but Rafe beat her to the punch.

"She'll be busy." His voice held quiet authority.

She glanced at her host, as did the customers in Fran's Diner who sat within hearing distance. "I will?" She didn't bother concealing the direct challenge in her question.

A reciprocating challenge sparked in Rafe's steel-gray eyes. "We're going to dinner at the Elk Lodge."

She affected complete surprise. "We are?"

He frowned at her. "Yeah, we are."

"How lovely." She turned her attention to Jason, who was waiting patiently for her and Rafe to hash out their misunderstanding. "I'm sorry, but I guess I already have other plans."

Jason grinned, though the gesture didn't completely disguise his regret. "I understand."

The young editor left the diner, and after a minute of speculative stares and silence, the people of Cedar Creek went back to their own business.

Lauren watched Rafe withdraw his leather billfold from the back pocket of his jeans and remove enough money to cover the check and leave a generous tip for Andrea. Leaning across the table, she kept her voice low. "You know, Dalton, we need to polish up your rusty dating skills. You were borderline barbaric just a minute ago. Has it been that long since you've asked a woman out on a date?"

"I never said it was a date."

She hid a grin. "Then what would you call it?"

"Going out and eating dinner cooked by someone other than you or myself."

She smirked, not believing him for a second. The man had been too possessive, jealous almost, at the thought of her accompanying Jason for an evening. "My, aren't you creative with your definitions."

He glared at her for that taunt, but his menacing scowl lacked conviction. She laughed and accepted his underhanded invitation to Friday night dinner at the Elk Lodge.

* * *

"That wasn't so awful with Jason, now, was it?"

Rafe glanced at the woman walking beside him as they approached Gentry's feed and supply store. Lauren's expression was femininely smug, the mischievous gleam in her eyes impetuous. He had the strongest urge to grin at her—she was so full of life and sass, she made him want to share in that infectious enthusiasm.

Restraining the spontaneous impulse, he averted his gaze to Chad, who skipped a few yards ahead of them, still basking in the glow of having made a new friend.

"You did most of the talking," Rafe replied, knowing she was the sole reason he'd managed to endure Jason's interview. The focus had been off him until Jason's final question.

A smile quirked the corner of her mouth as she gave him a sidelong glance. "Are you saying I dominated the conversation?"

"No, I'm saying that you made the morning bearable." That was the truth. He never would have lasted through those uncomfortable pleasantries and scrutinizing stares if he'd been alone. Her friendly, gregarious personality had diffused the town's reserve, and made him seem more approachable, too.

Lauren gently grasped his arm, stopping him before they reached the double glass doors leading into the feed store. Her touch, as innocent as it was, made his heart beat just a bit faster, made his blood run just a bit hotter.

He stared at her upturned face, her cheeks and nose pink from the sun, her blue eyes so incredibly serene they nearly stole his breath from his lungs.

"Rafe, what you said to Jason about why you're doing this for Chad..."

"Don't make a big deal out of it," he said abruptly before she could praise him for something he didn't deserve.

A slight frown marred her brows. "But—"

"No buts. What I said to Jason isn't up for further discussion." Especially when he was still coming to terms with how much Chad's visit was changing the solitary life he'd created for himself, how Lauren's presence made him question his future. He'd done more soul-searching in the past couple of days than he had in an entire year, and he found it difficult to dissect feelings and actions he didn't completely understand yet—emotions that were seemingly linked to this woman who made him want so many things and need even more.

She narrowed her gaze at him, more in frustration than anger. "You are *so* stubborn," she huffed.

His brows shot up in amusement. "Oh, that's laughable, coming from Miz Obstinate herself."

She made a face at him that scrunched up her nose in the most adorable way, and damn if he didn't almost laugh at her antics. He wanted to laugh so badly his chest ached to release the peculiar pressure, yet it was as though he'd forgotten how.

"Lauren! Rafe!"

His sister's voice snapped him out of his disturbing thoughts, saving him from contemplating the fact that his existence had become so dull and bleak that he couldn't even enjoy something as natural as laughter.

"Kristin!" Chad was the first to greet Rafe's sister as she exited the store with James behind her, a bag of feed slung over his shoulder. The boy ran up to the pair and gave them each a hug and started telling them all about how he'd eaten breakfast with his new friend, Randy, at Fran's Diner.

Once Chad's spiel ended, Kristin addressed Rafe and Lauren. ''Gentry had these flyers on the counter inside, and I picked one up, thinking this might be a fun outing for Chad.''

She extended the bright yellow piece of paper toward Rafe, but he couldn't bring himself to take it. Bold black print announced the annual Cody Nite Rodeo, with nightly events through August. Too many memories assailed him, and not many were pleasant ones. Tangled up with his last rodeo performance was the time he'd spent with his father at the Cody Rodeo when Rafe had been a youth.

No, the memories weren't ones he cared to resurrect.

''Why don't you and James take Chad?'' Rafe suggested abruptly.

Kristin glanced from Rafe to Lauren, her expression uncertain. ''Rafe, I think you should go with him—''

''No, Kristin.'' His tone was gruff and uncompromising. Too late, he noticed Lauren watching him. Too late, he realized his hand absently rubbed his injured thigh through his jeans.

Kristin sighed but didn't push the issue, though Rafe knew his sister was very aware of the source of his refusal. ''Fine.''

Chad's shoulders sagged in obvious disappointment, but he accepted the decision without a complaint.

James watched the boy's reaction, and something

warm and caring entered his gaze. "Would you mind if Kristin and I took Chad tomorrow afternoon to the Cody Rodeo?" he asked Lauren. "You could come along, too, if you'd like."

Lauren cupped Chad's chin in her palm and smiled into the boy's expectant face. "You know what, I think it would be wonderful if the two of you took Chad to the rodeo, though I think I'll stay behind and keep Rafe company."

Rafe opened his mouth to refute that last comment, but decided against an argument he more than likely wouldn't win, anyway.

"I'll see if Sally and her husband can come along, too, so Chad can pal around with Randy," Kristin suggested, which earned an excited yeah from Chad.

While his sister, James and Lauren worked out the details for tomorrow's adventure, Rafe excused himself and entered the feed store, trying not to think of all the possibilities of spending the day alone with Lauren.

Lauren glanced over the top of her book toward the stables, hoping to catch a glimpse of Rafe. Kristin and James had arrived over two hours ago to pick up Chad and take him to the rodeo, and she'd spent the time sitting on the front porch reading her novel, debating whether to go see what Rafe was up to or leave him alone.

Ever since yesterday's incident at the feed store he'd been moody and distant. Unapproachable, but not as rude as he'd once been. There was a specific reason he'd refused to take Chad to the Cody Nite Rodeo, and Lauren couldn't help but mull over the problem.

Giving him time alone to brood was probably the smartest thing, but Lauren had never been one to play it safe or ignore a challenge. Rafe, with all his dark secrets and his gruff attitude, intrigued her, mainly because she knew the man harbored a wealth of hurt and guilt that would destroy him if he didn't deal with his personal pain. She'd seen too many glimpses of a gentler side to Rafe to believe he wasn't anything but a good, honest man who deserved to be happy.

She wanted to see him happy and tried not to analyze too deeply why that seemed so important to her.

Giving up on her novel, she headed inside. In the kitchen, she fixed a couple of sandwiches and gathered together a cluster of grapes and a handful of the homemade cookies Kristin had sent home with them Sunday evening. She found a small carton in the pantry, packed her goods, added two cold cans of soda and tucked the box beneath her arm, then headed toward the stables.

She found Rafe in the back office, head bent over a journal opened on his desk, lost in the sea of paperwork spread out around him. His dark hair fell over his brow. He'd rolled up the sleeves of his chambray shirt to reveal strong, tanned forearms. Though he was deep in concentration, he seemed at ease in this environment, relaxed, even…and incredibly sexy.

She could have watched him all afternoon, just like this, could have let the pleasant warmth spilling through her veins and the slow, delicious awakening of desire unfurling within her go on and on.…

Shaking off those sensations before they got her

into trouble, she knocked on the door frame. He glanced up, something between surprise and that frustrating reserve of his passing over his features. He didn't scowl, which she took as an encouraging sign that her presence wasn't entirely unwelcome.

She stepped into his office, too aware of his gaze lingering on her bare legs. She'd worn shorts and a tank top today, and though there was nothing revealing about either article of clothing, the heat in his eyes seemed to singe her right through the material.

She shifted on her sandaled feet and gestured toward the box. "Since you haven't eaten anything since breakfast, I thought you might be hungry."

Leaning back in his chair, he folded his hands over his flat belly, his aloofness ebbing into something far more seductive. "Yeah, I seem to have developed a sudden appetite," he murmured.

A distinct tingle shot through her at his double entendre. "Ah, good. Got a blanket?" She nearly cringed—when had their conversation taken on such a sexual slant?

"A blanket?" Male interest glimmered in his eyes. "What for?"

"I was thinking we could spread it out beneath the tree right outside the stables and eat there."

He didn't move, but kept her trapped within his stormy, reckless gaze. "Why can't we just eat in my office?"

"Because it's too *stuffy* in here," she said meaningfully.

The corners of his mouth twitched with a hint of humor, but he didn't follow through with that teasing promise. He never did.

She sighed, a long-drawn-out sound bordering on impatience. "Come on, Rafe. It's a gorgeous day, and I'm sure you could use the break from all this tedious paperwork."

He said nothing, though she could sense him wavering.

"Don't make me beg for your company, Dalton."

"No, I don't suppose that would be a pretty sight." He stood and rounded his desk. "You win. Outside it is."

A few minutes later they were sitting beneath a shade tree on an old, soft blanket Rafe had retrieved from a shelf in the tack room. She sat with her legs crossed while Rafe opted to stretch out. A pleasant breeze blew, fluttering the ends of her ponytail along her neck.

She handed him two ham and cheese sandwiches, garnished with lettuce and tomatoes. He unwrapped the first one and took a big bite, then chewed heartily.

Enjoying Rafe's ravenous appetite, Lauren popped open both cans of soda and set them in the empty box so they wouldn't topple over. Then she reached for a sandwich and pulled off the plastic wrap.

"So, why didn't you want to go to the Cody Rodeo today?" she asked conversationally, then filled her mouth with succulent ham and tangy cheese.

His robust chewing stopped, and his gaze gleamed with instant suspicion. She'd been prepared for hostility for her blatant prying, yet it never materialized. It amazed her how much he'd changed from the first day she'd met him. He had the potential to be the kind of charming man a woman could fall real hard for, as he'd been before his accident.

Shaking his head in mock disgust, he took a drink of his soda to wash down the bite in his mouth. "I should have guessed there was an ulterior motive to you bringing me food and suggesting this cozy picnic."

She didn't deny his accusation. "You can't blame me for wondering."

He tried hard to look irritated, but fell short of the mark. "You don't leave anything alone, do you?"

"I like solving puzzles, and you, Rafe Dalton, are one big mystery." She opened the bag of grapes and popped one into her mouth. "Now tell me why."

He polished off his first sandwich and shrugged, the movement stiffer than it should have been. "All that walking would have taken a toll on my leg."

A slow, knowing smile claimed her mouth. "Liar."

His lips flattened in exasperation. He obviously hadn't expected her to call him on his convenient excuse.

"Tell me the truth, Rafe," she encouraged softly. "Please?"

"Why does this matter so much to you?"

Because I care and I want to know everything about you—who you were and why you've become the man you are. "I just think if you talk about whatever it is that's bothering you, you might feel better."

He cast her a dubious look.

"It seems to work for the kids I deal with."

A caustic sound erupted from his throat. "I'm a grown man, Lauren."

"Who carries a lot of blame and guilt for something that isn't necessarily your fault," she replied pointedly. "Same difference."

He didn't reply, just averted his gaze to something in the distant pasture, his entire body tense. Calmly, she finished her sandwich, waiting for him to direct their conversation. More than anything, she wanted this man to open up and trust her with his darkest secrets, but she refused to pressure him further. The next move would be up to him.

Her patience was rewarded. Very quietly, he said, "Not only haven't I been to a rodeo since my accident, the Cody Rodeo holds a lot of memories for me."

"Good memories?"

"Mixed in with some bad," he admitted, plucking a few grapes from the stem and tossing them into his mouth.

When he didn't elaborate, she prompted him. "Tell me."

"The Cody Rodeo is where I first competed as a young boy, or rather, where my father pushed me to compete when I really wasn't ready to," he finally said. "My dad rode, too, except he was never good enough to claim the championship, so that became his obsession with me."

She drew her knees up and wrapped her arms around her legs. "It was up to you to live his dream for him?"

"Yep. And the thing was, I *wanted* to please my father, and since it seemed the only way I could do that was to compete and win, claiming the PRCA title became my sole obsession. A very destructive one." His tone dripped self-disgust.

Lauren handed Rafe a chocolate chip cookie, which he accepted, then took one for herself. "What did your mother have to say about you competing?"

"She was a quiet woman and never questioned my father's decisions. She died of pneumonia when I was twelve." He glanced at her, his eyes reflecting pain and sorrow. "My father was so intent on competing, and winning, that we were on the road traveling the circuit when we should have been home for my mother and Kristin. It took a phone call from Kristin begging us to come home because my mother was so sick before my father finally agreed. We made it to my mother's bedside the day before she died." He shook his head in silent admonishment. "I was so caught up in my father's fixation to win that I neglected what should have been the most important thing in my life. Taking care of my mom and sister."

"You were just a kid yourself."

His features twisted with resentment. "My selfishness didn't end there, Lauren. My father didn't take but a few days to mourn my mother's passing before we were on the road again, on to the next rodeo, leaving Kristin behind with a good family friend to wait for our sporadic visits. We had a schedule to keep, fees that had been paid, and there wasn't anything that was going to distract my father from that agenda."

A lump gathered in her throat at the young, confused boy he'd been. "And so you kept on competing?" she asked quietly, suspecting there was more.

"Yeah, my father kept on pushing, and I kept on competing when I should have been at home taking care of my sister on a full-time basis." He reached for another cookie and reclined on his side on the blanket, looking at her. "And you know what the irony of all this is? My father wanted me to take the championship, but I didn't win the PRCA title until after he died of a heart attack."

She offered him a gentle smile, hoping to offset the bitterness suddenly swirling in the air between them. "Your championship title is still something to be proud of."

"You think so?" He held her gaze for a long second, seemingly contemplating his self-worth. "I paid a steep price for that title, and nearly killed myself and another rider. That's hardly something to be proud of." He scrubbed an agitated hand through his thick hair and gave a self-deprecating laugh. "I inherited those same demanding, aggressive, selfish traits I came to despise in my father. I hated what my old man did to me, but his lessons were so ingrained, I pressured a kid to get on a deadly bull before he was ready."

Lauren's throat tightened, and for once, she felt at a loss for words to soothe such deep pain.

With a long, harsh sigh, he rolled to his back, folded his hands beneath his head and stared at the few clouds dotting the blue sky. "And you know what the worst part is? I don't trust myself with kids anymore, and I can only imagine what kind of father I'd be. All I know about love and discipline is what my father taught me, which isn't something I want to pass on to a child of my own." His big body shuddered, and he squeezed his eyes shut, as if to block the awful thought. "And dammit, I'm no hero!" he muttered gruffly.

Lauren hugged her legs tighter to her chest, hurting for Rafe way deep inside, for the lonely boy he'd been and the cynical man he'd become. She ached to tell him he'd be a kind, caring father, but knew he'd never believe her. But she could make him forget all the burdens he carried, just for a little while. She gave in to the impulse to lean over and kiss him very softly on his lips.

His eyes opened, and before she could back away, his hand reached out and curled around her neck, keeping her face inches from his. "What was that for?" His voice was low and raspy and very curious.

She touched her tongue to her bottom lip, suddenly nervous. "I like the way kissing you makes me feel. Warm. Excited. Eager for more." Her reckless honesty, and the male heat in his eyes, caused her face to flush, but she didn't hold back. "Do you feel something, too?"

A faintly proprietary light entered his gaze, and Lauren's heart gave a distinct thump in her chest. Then, abruptly, he let her go and stood, breaking the seductive spell that had gripped them both. "I've got paperwork to do," he said, not looking at her. "Thank you for lunch."

Lauren watched Rafe walk toward the stables, a withering sensation settling in her belly. Stubborn man. Just as he refused to deal with his past, he was equally unwilling to acknowledge the growing feelings between them.

CHAPTER SEVEN

RAFE'S stomach tumbled with nerves and anticipation. No matter how many times he tried to tell himself the gift he was about to give Lauren was out of concern for her soft, smooth skin getting burned, his heart wasn't fully convinced of his noble gesture. The woman's Stetson he'd bought for her served a dual purpose, and a selfish one, at that. Ultimately, he wanted to see that radiant smile of hers that never failed to warm the cold, lonely part of his soul, and he enjoyed witnessing her unabashed delight, and the way her blue eyes lit up with pleasure over the simplest things.

A tiny frown formed on his brow as he headed through the living room to the front porch, where he knew Lauren was enjoying her morning cup of coffee. He wasn't sure when her vibrancy and capricious nature had become such an important part of his day, yet every morning when he woke, she was the first thing he thought of. And during the day, she consumed his thoughts, too. The nights were the worst, because he'd remember her kisses, her gentle touch, and his desire for her would keep him tossing and turning until dawn.

The woman tied him up in knots like nobody ever had, and though he knew what he was beginning to feel for this woman went into dangerous territory, he craved everything about her—her generosity, her warmth and her beauty that went deeper than her features.

Stopping at the screen door, he indulged in a quiet, private moment of looking at her, enjoying the gentle serenity that claimed her expression as she sipped from the mug in her hands and gazed at the horses in the pasture. She stood by the porch railing wearing a pink T-shirt and a pair of jeans that molded to her sleek curves and long legs. Today, she wore her hair down, and the ends curled ever so slightly along her shoulders.

Desire and longing rumbled through him before he could stop the reaction. She looked like she belonged here, on his ranch and in his life. Realizing the impossibility of those thoughts, he firmly banned them from his mind, along with the feelings she evoked in him. Lauren didn't belong in the country. She led a fast-paced life in the city, working at a job she loved. Three more days and she'd be gone from Cedar Creek and his life, and he'd have nothing but memories.

He pushed open the screen door and stepped onto the porch. She turned at the sound of his booted steps, greeting him with one of her breath-stealing smiles.

"I just love it here," she said with a soft sigh. "It's so quiet and peaceful and gorgeous. Especially in the morning."

Moving closer to her, he slid his fingers over the brim of the hat he held in his hands. "I'm sure your favorable impression of Wyoming would change come winter. They can be pretty long and harsh, not to mention dealing with a whole lot of confinement during blizzards and storms."

"Depends on who and what you're confined with," she said with a whole lot of sass and enough sensual insinuation to make his blood heat at the possibilities. She took another drink of coffee, her gaze dropping to the beige Stetson he held. "Did you get yourself a new hat?"

Feeling suddenly awkward, he thrust the gift toward her. "No, I bought it for you."

She glanced from the hat to his face but didn't take the present he offered. "You did?" Her voice was breathless with expectation.

He nodded jerkily and affected concern. "That delicate skin of yours is going to turn to leather if you're not careful about protecting it."

That lovely smile he'd hoped for made its appearance, making his insides tighten and his heart hammer in his chest. She set her cup of coffee on the railing and took the hat, sliding her fingers over the soft beaver pelt. "Wow, my very own Stetson. Does this make me a genuine cowgirl?"

"At least for three more days."

Her smile faltered a bit at his reminder of how soon she'd be leaving, making him wonder if she dreaded Sunday's arrival as much as he was beginning to. She'd not only captivated him, but she'd charmed the residents of Cedar Creek with her sunny disposition and generous heart. He'd gone into town yesterday afternoon to purchase her Stetson while she and Chad were visiting with Kristin, Sally and Randy. Quite a few people had approached him to comment on Lauren and how much they liked her. From there, conversations evolved to his participation in Chad's wish and admiration for his unselfish gesture. Though it had been difficult to accept the praise after everything he'd put the townsfolk of Cedar Creek through, he felt as though a fragile truce had developed between him and the town he'd alienated with his gruff temperament and unsociable mood.

This woman was the sole reason for the drastic change in his attitude. She knew every contemptible thing about him yet refused to believe the worst. Somehow, she managed to turn every argument about his dark reputation against him, until he'd begun to believe that maybe he'd judged himself, and his actions, too harshly.

"So, what do you think?"

The sound of Lauren's voice pulled Rafe to the woman standing in front of him. She was now wearing the beige Stetson he'd bought for her. He thought she looked incredibly beautiful, achingly so. "It's a perfect fit," he said, pushing the brim back so he could see her sparkling eyes and put this moment in his memory.

"Thank you for the hat," she said, and tentatively stepped toward him. With one hand resting on his chest, she kissed him lightly on the cheek.

A shaft of heat and awareness zinged through his veins, making him remember the words she'd spoken two days ago that were never far from his mind. *I like the way kissing you makes me feel. Warm. Excited. Eager for more. Do you feel something, too?*

He hadn't issued a reply to her question because his answer had scared the hell out of him. Oh, yeah, he felt something, too—that same excitement and eagerness she'd mentioned, and a need that transcended physical desires. He wanted Lauren Richmond, but the emotional hunger he felt for her couldn't be appeased with a mere kiss. That particular craving went deeper than anything he'd ever experienced for a woman.

Yet he knew if they pursued the mutual desire growing between them, it would only complicate matters. Three more days, and she'd be gone from his life, back to California where she belonged. She'd move on to her next foster case, date one of the eligible, more qualified men her mother set her up with and forget all about him, as it should be.

The lecture, as sound as it was, did nothing to diminish how badly he wanted to carry this woman off to his bed and make love to her until he had her out of his system. Except he suspected a few quick tumbles wouldn't be enough. He feared once he had her in that sensual, all-consuming way, he'd be forever addicted to her brand of loving.

And he'd never be the same again.

"Hey, Rafe," Chad said as he came out onto the porch wearing the new leather chaps Kristin and James had bought for him at the Cody Rodeo. "You promised to show me how to rope just like the cowboys do it at the Cody Rodeo. Can we do that this morning?"

Grateful for the interruption, Rafe addressed Chad. "Yep, I did make that promise, didn't I?" He inclined his head toward Lauren. "You up for a roping lesson?"

"Absolutely," she said, giving Chad a wink.

They headed down to an empty paddock, and Rafe retrieved two coiled ropes from the tack room. He met his avid students in the warm sunshine and handed one length of rope to Chad.

"Kinda hard to rope a calf when you don't have

any,'' Lauren teased, sliding her hands into the back pockets of her jeans.

His mouth twitched with the humor he was hard-pressed to hold back lately. ''We can use that empty barrel over there, and other props. Trust me,'' he drawled lazily, ''you're gonna have a hard enough time roping something that's stationary.''

Rafe spent the next hour patiently teaching Chad and Lauren how to build a small loop, then keep it circling and steady enough to toss over the barrel. Before long, Chad managed to make a few attempts that landed short of the mark.

''Good try,'' Rafe said, praising the boy so intent on roping the barrel. ''It's all in your wrist. Just keep it relaxed and let the rope out a little at a time until you feel comfortable throwing it.''

''This is hard work,'' Lauren grumbled good-naturedly, shaking out her tired arm. Perspiration put a sheen on her flushed face and made her eyes appear deep blue. ''I think I need a break. How about a cool drink, you two?''

''I'll take a lemonade, please,'' Chad said, his gaze narrowed on his target as he concentrated on roping the barrel. The boy looked tired but too determined to quit.

Rafe took the rope from her. ''Quitting already?'' he taunted, wanting to see the sassy side of this woman.

On cue, she thrust her chin out with a mixture of stubbornness and feminine pride. ''Hey, this Stetson only gives me the appearance of a cowgirl. Unfortunately, it doesn't have any magical powers to *make* me one.'' She wrinkled her nose at him. ''Now refreshments, I can handle.'' With a grin, she headed toward the gate leading out of the paddock.

Rafe began building himself a loop, letting out rope until it made a nice size circle. ''Before you go, would you mind uprighting that hay bale over there?'' he asked pleasantly.

She stopped in her tracks and glanced to where he motioned with his head. Seeing that both Chad and Rafe had their hands full, she nodded. ''Oh, sure.''

Rafe watched her head toward the far side of the paddock, enjoying the gentle, natural sway of her hips as she walked. Out of the corner of his mouth, he whispered to Chad, ''What do you say we rope ourselves a filly?''

Understanding dawned as Chad followed Rafe's line of vision to Lauren, who was bending over to reposition the hay bale. A huge grin transformed Chad's expression, and his eyes lit up with mischief. ''Yeah,'' he whispered, lowering his own rope to watch Rafe's skills.

''How's that?'' Lauren asked, turning to face the two of them.

''Perfect,'' he said, moving slowly closer. ''Now just stand real still and be good....''

He didn't expect her to obey, and she didn't. For every step he took forward, she took two to the side, her gaze filling with instant suspicion. ''Rafe, what do you think you're doing?''

The rope whirled in a growing loop at his side, rising higher and higher. ''Why, I'm gonna lasso myself a spirited filly.''

She gasped indignantly, though the playful twinkle in her eyes told him she'd be a good sport. ''You wouldn't!''

He lifted a dark brow. "Wouldn't I?" he challenged mildly.

"Well, don't expect me to stand still and make it easy on you!" She darted across the paddock in an attempt to thwart him.

"Nope, that wouldn't be any fun at all." He kept his stride deceptively lazy and nonthreatening, which only served to heighten the anticipation of what was to come—Lauren's capture. "Pay attention, Chad," he directed in a low, soothing tone. "Keep your eyes on your quarry, and try to calculate their next move. Watch their legs to get a feel for which way they plan to sprint." His gaze dropped to those long, sexy limbs. Her booted feet were apart, but her left knee, bent very slightly, gave away her next advance, which he easily countered.

She let out a sound of frustration and waggled a finger at him. "I'm gonna get even with you for this, Rafe Dalton."

His loop continued to twirl as he let the anticipation of being caught intensify. "Oh, I do hope so, Miz Richmond," he drawled, imagining the different ways she'd take retribution.

Gradually, he maneuvered her into a fenced-in corner. Though a good ten yards separated them, he had her trapped, and she knew it, too. Awareness made her breathing quicken and heated excitement flared in her eyes as she searched for a means of escape. Her full breasts rose and fell enticingly. His gaze was drawn to the arousing sight.

His breathing grew a little deeper, too, and his belly tightened with irrepressible need and desire for this feisty woman.

"Lasso her, Rafe!" Chad urged gleefully, reminding Rafe that he and Lauren weren't alone as he suddenly wished they were. Somehow, what had started as an amusing game had become a slow, tantalizing seduction, one he wanted to take to its inevitable conclusion.

Easing closer, he flicked his wrist to steady the loop, ready to claim his prize. "Easy now," he murmured in the low, husky voice that never failed to calm a skittish horse. Lauren, however, knew better than to trust him.

She dampened her bottom lip with her tongue and feinted to the left. When he automatically swayed in that direction to block her, she bolted to the right with a triumphant "Ha!" and made a beeline for the gate. Quickly recovering, he sent the loop sailing…right over the top of her head and around her body. The rope tightened around her waist and pinned her arms to her sides, stopping her mid-sprint without jerking her off her feet.

He allowed enough slack so as not to hurt her and gave her time to steady herself. "Now that's how it's done, Chad," Rafe said, deliberately smug.

She gaped at him in shock, as if she couldn't believe he'd actually truss her up like a calf. "Very funny, Dalton." She squirmed to edge the rope up past her elbows so she could slip it over her head, but with no success. "You can let me go now."

"Naw, I kinda like you just like this." He pulled her leisurely, inexorably toward him, despite the paltry struggles he suspected were for Chad's benefit. "Well, we caught our filly, Chad. Think we can tame her?"

She tossed her head and sent a mock glare his way that belied the smile teasing the corners of her mouth.

"You're gonna have your hands full with this filly, cowboy."

He rolled his eyes. "Don't I know it." He kept reeling her in, tamping the laughter threatening to rumble from his chest. And then there was the grin he was hard-pressed to suppress, too. God, when was the last time he'd had such simple, nonsensical fun? He couldn't remember, but planned to enjoy this moment while it lasted.

He thumbed his hat back, meeting her spitfire gaze. "I'm having second thoughts about letting you loose."

A few feet away, she abruptly stopped, awe transforming her features. "Why, Rafe Dalton, is that a *smile* I detect on your face?"

He quickly schooled his expression, but knew the merriment he refused to let form on his lips shone in his eyes. "Why, Miz Richmond, I haven't the faintest idea what you're talking about."

She laughed in disbelief, the sound light, sweet and filled with levity, cajoling him to join in the playful moment. Gently, he tugged on the rope, and she stumbled forward those last couple of steps. Realizing she couldn't use her hands should she lose her balance, he caught her against his chest, banding his arm around her back to support her. Too late, he discovered his mistake. His noble gesture put her mouth mere inches from his and aligned their bodies perfectly. His responded accordingly to her soft curves, and he battled against the instinctive male reaction.

She grinned, her gaze traveling from his lips to his eyes. "Maybe it's been so long that you've forgotten what it's like to smile, but from my vantage point, that's exactly what it looks like to me.''

Rafe opened his mouth to refute her opinion, but the sound of an approaching vehicle caught Chad's attention, and he ran to the fence to see who the visitor was. Rafe knew he should release Lauren, yet he was helpless to listen to that voice of reason, not when all he could think about was kissing the lips so close to his he could feel her warm, ragged breath.

''Kristin is here!'' Chad announced, and waved wildly at the truck Rafe couldn't see from where he and Lauren were standing. Rafe heard Chad exit the paddock, then the sound of a car door slamming shut, and still he didn't move, couldn't have if his life depended on it.

She swallowed, and he watched her regain her composure. ''Are you going to let me go,'' she whispered, ''or am I going to be totally humiliated in front of your sister when she sees me all trussed up like this?''

That snapped him out of his sensual fog, and he put the necessary distance between them, for propriety's sake, as well as his sanity.

''Could you, ah, help me loosen the rope?'' she asked tentatively, indicating her constrained arms. ''I can't reach the knot.''

His gaze lowered to where the slipknot rested just below her breasts. Realizing what the task entailed, he forced himself to lift unsteady hands. He fumbled with the tightened rope, unable to help the way his knuckles brushed the undersides of that soft fullness as he worked on the knot. Apparently, neither could she prevent the swelling of her breasts or the way her nipples drew into hard beads against her cotton shirt.

Heat coiled low in his belly, spreading outward to every nerve ending. Averting his gaze to her face didn't help cool his ardor, not when her expression reflected the same vital hunger that twisted through him.

As soon as the rope gave way and fell to her feet, he stepped away from her and eased a taut breath between his teeth. Swearing at the futility of the situation and this mystifying need he had for her, he turned to head into the stables until his body settled enough to greet his sister.

"Rafe?"

Her soft voice beckoned to him, and he stopped against his better judgment and glanced back. "Yeah?" His voice was rough with the frustration coursing through his blood.

She blinked at him, something warm and mischievous glimmering in her crystal-blue eyes. "Just for the record, you smiled."

Damned if he didn't experience the urge to grin at her satisfied expression. He bit the inside of his cheek. "Did not."

"Did, too," she argued mildly. "And before I leave on Sunday, I'll prove there's more where that came from."

Lauren relaxed in Rafe's embrace as they danced to the slow country ballad the band was playing at Cedar Creek's finest steak house. The Elk Lodge was filled with Friday night patrons, and though she and Rafe had received curious looks when they'd arrived for dinner, after the initial interest the inquisitive stares and idle comments had ebbed. A few people stopped by to ask where Chad was, and Lauren explained that he was with Kristin and James. The couple had asked if Chad could spent the night at their place, and her young charge had begged and pleaded until she'd laughingly agreed.

Knowing Chad had only a few more days left to enjoy his vacation, Lauren found it difficult to refuse him anything.

She and Rafe ate their dinner around easy conversation, and instead of leaving after they'd finished their meal as Lauren fully expected Rafe to suggest, they'd sat and talked some more, about inconsequential things, really, but everything he said captured her attention and gave her a deeper insight into Rafe the man.

Despite his low personal opinion of his character, beneath those tough layers of guilt and recrimination she discovered the kind, caring cowboy Chad had met a few years ago…and found herself falling for him. Deeply and irrevocably. What had begun as a quest to soothe the savage beast she'd met over two weeks ago had turned her emotions topsy-turvy. When she looked at Rafe, she felt things that surpassed physical attraction and desire. Oh, sure, she experienced a heart-pounding excitement when he was near, and when she looked into his smoky, sexy eyes, she couldn't stop the melting sensation in the pit of her stomach. Yet there was more, that indefinable something that had always been lacking in the men she'd dated in the past—a warmth, a connection, a sense of rightness.

Is this the love I've been searching for? she wondered, shaken by the thought.

Rafe rubbed a gentle hand along her back. "Hey, are you okay?"

Clearing her mind of the startling revelation, she summoned a smile that faltered on her lips. "I'm fine."

He didn't look convinced as he maneuvered them around a couple two-stepping across the dance floor. "Are you having a good time? We can leave if you want."

"I'm having a wonderful time," she said truthfully, not wanting the night to end. "Though I thought this wasn't supposed to be a date."

His eyes crinkled at the corners in amusement. "It's not."

She couldn't resist teasing him. Goading a smile from him had become a playful battle of wills between them, one she couldn't wait to win. "Well, we are dancing together. Real close." The friction of their chests, bellies and thighs flooded her body with enough heat to start a wildfire beneath the surface of her skin.

"Dancing was your idea, not mine," he pointed out.

The fingers resting at the back of his neck inched upward, touching the thick, silky strands of his hair. "I don't remember you putting up much of an argument."

He made a sound between humor and skepticism. "Like I'd win an argument with you."

"You've got a point," she conceded with a sassy grin, and gave the debate more thought. "Certainly you being romantic qualifies this as a date."

"I'm not doing anything romantic at all." A muscular thigh slid between hers, aligning their bodies closer, if that was possible.

Her pulse quickened. "Depends on whose definition of romantic."

"Go ahead," he drawled. "Enlighten me on *your* definition."

"Well, you've been *very* attentive this evening."

"We've got an avid audience, and I want to make a good impression."

Laughter bubbled from her throat. "We both know what a bald-faced lie that is!"

He shrugged, admitting nothing.

"And what about the way you're holding me while we're dancing? Or the fact that you've been staring at my mouth like you want to kiss me." His eyes had darkened to charcoal, and in a whisper-soft voice only he could hear she said, "I'd let you kiss me, you know."

She could feel his heart beating erratically against her breast, as crazily as her own. He looked like he was seriously considering the idea. Then the music changed to an upbeat country song, forcing them to shuffle faster across the dance floor or get trampled by enthusiastic two-steppers.

The moment was lost to the fast-paced, rollicking music, but the sensual tension shimmering between them remained long after they'd left the Elk Lodge and headed home.

A comfortable silence settled in the cab of Rafe's truck, the only sound coming from the radio, which was tuned into a country station. Lauren stared out the passenger window and gasped when a bolt of lightning streaked across the night sky, illuminating the interior of the vehicle.

"Looks like we're in for a storm tonight," Rafe commented, his voice low and sexy in the close confines of the truck. "Hopefully we'll beat it home."

No sooner were those words out of his mouth than a fat drop of rain splattered on the windshield. Then another, and another, until he had no choice but to put on the wipers so he could see. By the time he brought his truck to a stop in his driveway, the rain fell steadily.

Rafe scowled at the elements and the fact that the storm couldn't have waited another few minutes, until he and Lauren were safe and dry inside the house. "Looks like we'll have to make a run for the porch."

He shut off the truck, but before he could pull the keys from the ignition, Lauren's hand closed over his, stopping him. He met her gaze in silent question.

Even in the dim cab he could see the reckless daring glowing in her eyes. He didn't have to wait long to find out what fanciful idea had spawned in that beautiful head of hers.

Her fingers trailed lightly up his arm, and she leaned close, her mouth kicking up in a tempting smile. "Leave the radio on and dance with me."

CHAPTER EIGHT

RAFE shook his head, certain her words had somehow gotten distorted by the soft patter of rain against
the hood of his truck. "Excuse me?"

"I said, leave the radio on and dance with me."

Nope, he hadn't misunderstood her. "In the rain?"
He frowned at the ridiculous suggestion. "Are you
crazy?"

"We're going to get soaked anyway," she rea-
soned. "So what's the difference?"

His hands tightened on the steering wheel as he
tried to envision himself frolicking in the rain. He
couldn't picture it. The thought defied logic. "You
are crazy."

"Come on, Rafe," she cajoled, sweet as honey.
"Nobody will see us, and I promise not to tell a soul
that we played in the rain."

Before he could issue another objection, she
slipped from the truck into the warm, summer rain.
She stood in front of his headlights, which he hadn't
turned off yet, her arms open wide and her face lifted
toward the night sky as she spun around. The beams
of light silhouetted her body and made the drops of
rain falling on her hair and face sparkle like dia-
monds. Pure male heat rumbled through him as the
front of her dress grew damp, clinging to her breasts,
waist and legs.

Then he heard her light, melodious laughter, and
the flirtatious sound beckoned to him, awakening that

132

lonely, aching part of him that craved this woman's tenderness. The tide of emotion washing over him should have had him throwing up blockades, yet he welcomed the warmth and succumbed to the need to let go of past burdens just for tonight.

"What the hell," he muttered. Leaving the keys in the ignition, he cranked up the radio. Then he exited the vehicle, strode toward her and caught her in his arms, pulling their bodies intimately close. He eased into a fast-paced two-step, and she easily kept time, her sandaled feet staying in sync with his as he maneuvered her around his truck.

"Where did you learn to two-step?" he asked as the rain dampened his hair and saturated his shirt. Despite his earlier protests, he was having fun. "I would have thought you'd be a waltzer."

"Shows you just how much you need to learn about me," she said in that impudent way of hers. "And for the record, I do know how to waltz, which was a prerequisite for my debutante ball, but my roommate and I like to go country dancing." Grinning with infectious enthusiasm, she said, "Twirl me, Rafe."

He spun her around while holding her hand, then tugged her into his embrace and whirled them together, around and around, until she was laughing breathlessly. The rain drenched their hair and clothing, and water dripped from his nose and her chin, adding to the humorous situation.

And then it happened. That excruciating pressure in his chest he'd suppressed for too long broke free, and a deep rumble of laughter escaped him. The rusty chuckles mingled with Lauren's mirth until the sound developed the rich, male undertones he remembered from long ago.

The emotional release felt so good, so exhilarating, and he didn't want the joyful moment to end. Didn't want to let this incredible woman go, because she held the key to the darkest part of his soul.

The thought of his life without Lauren in it brought his feet to a sudden stop. He stared at her upturned face, her guileless smile, and his stomach pitched with so many uncertainties. He wanted her so badly he ached with the need, yet he had nothing to offer her beyond this one night.

The music played on and the rain continued to fall in a light drizzle as they stood there for what could have been minutes or hours, he couldn't be sure. Lifting his hand, he pushed wet strands of hair off her face, intending to let her go after that brief brush of his fingertips along her silky skin. Except one caress led to another, and then touching her was no longer enough. And when she closed her eyes and her body trembled against his, he lost all sense of time or reason.

Delving his hands into her hair, he tilted her head and kissed her, tasting the rain on her lips and reveling in the way her mouth opened for a deeper union. He stroked his tongue along hers, hot and eager, and felt fire lick through him. With a helpless groan, he gathered her in his arms, holding her tight, and she slipped her arms around his neck to get closer still.

Her breasts swelled and strained against his chest, and a soft, mewling sound slipped from her throat. Passion rose swiftly, and neither one of them denied the torrent of sensations that had been building between them the past week.

The rain should have cooled them down, but he was burning up with a fever that began and ended with Lauren. His hands roamed restlessly down her back, and the desperate kiss he gave her spoke the words he couldn't bring himself to say. *I want to make love to you.*

Her uninhibited response and soft moan of acquiescence gave him the answer he sought. *Yes.*

Reluctantly, he lifted his mouth from hers, ending the kiss. No words were necessary, and none were spoken as he shut off the truck and retrieved his keys, then took her hand. Together they dashed toward the porch and into the house. He didn't stop until they were in his darkened bedroom, and only then did he give her time to change her mind.

"We're dripping all over the floor," she whispered after a long, silent moment passed.

He heard the tremor of nervousness in her voice, a touch of vulnerability he understood because he felt it, too. But there was nothing to indicate a change of heart, and he felt at once relieved and very anxious to feel her bare skin against his.

"Maybe we should take off our wet clothes," he suggested huskily, and slowly undid the first three buttons on the front of her damp dress, his need for her running hot and molten through his veins. His fingers stroked the soft, flawless skin he revealed, then he smoothed his flattened palm inside the opening, seeking the warm, resilient flesh of her breast.

She caught his wrist and stopped him before he reached his goal. Beneath his hand, her heart beat erratically.

She drew a shaky breath. "Before we go any further, I need something from you, Rafe."

In the darkness, his gaze searched hers, hoping, praying that she wouldn't ask for promises he couldn't give her. "And what's that?"

She lifted her free hand and skimmed her fingertips along his jaw. "A smile. Just for me."

Obliging her request wasn't as difficult as he thought it might be. All he had to do was remember this woman playing in the rain, her laughter, her joy for life, and his lips gradually curved into a genuine smile, just for her.

Her breath caught, her eyes glowing with delight and wonder. "You are, by far, one of the sexiest men I've ever met." Sighing reverently, she touched his mouth, tracing the shape of his lips. "And this smile, well, it makes me feel restless and very, very excited."

His grin deepened. "Yeah?"

"Oh, yeah." Her voice lowered to a husky purr, and she moved closer, twining her arms around his neck. Her body rubbed against his, their wet clothing a frustrating barrier. "It makes me want to kiss you." Bringing his mouth to hers, she did just that, branding him with a passionate kiss that made his head spin and his knees go weak.

Too soon, she lifted her lips from his, but her mouth quickly found other enticements. She tasted the skin along his jaw and neck. "And kissing you makes me want you," she murmured near his ear as her hands quickly undid the buttons of his shirt, then pulled the hem from the waistband of his jeans. "And wanting you makes me ache to touch you all over."

Her slender hands glided over his bare chest and down his belly, then began unbuckling his belt. He groaned helplessly as his body responded, growing hard and eager. Damn, he'd meant to seduce her, but the woman had her own agenda. And who was he to hamper her very arousing efforts?

What could have been an awkward situation—struggling to remove their drenched, clinging clothes—Lauren turned into a playful, sensual game. Laughter filled his bedroom, which he hadn't expected, not here and now when they were both on the verge of something more intimate. Yet the connection between them felt good and right, and now that she'd pried laughter and smiles from him, he found he wanted to share them with her, and more.

As each article of clothing dropped to the floor, they touched and teased and explored until the heat they generated dried their skin and made them both feverish with need. Rafe caressed her full breasts, then dipped his head to gently lave her nipples with his tongue. She tangled her fingers in his hair and sighed with unabashed pleasure.

His hands roamed, skimming her sleek curves, and when he found an especially sensitive spot at the indentation of her waist, she gasped and squirmed away. The bed behind her clipped the back of her knees, and she fell on top of the soft mattress. Joining her on the bed, he chuckled at her surprise and couldn't resist tickling her again.

Before long, they were breathless with laughter, and Lauren was begging him to stop the torture. He did, and all humor ceased as they both became aware of their very intimate position. Rafe's hard, muscular length trapped Lauren's soft, feminine body beneath him. Skin against heated, flushed skin, their arms and legs entwined so the slightest movement produced an electric, exquisite sensation.

Her lashes fell, and she rocked her hips against his. "Rafe..."

He groaned harshly, hating to leave her for even a second, but he did so to protect himself, and her. When he returned, she was just as pliant, just as welcoming. Sliding between her parted legs, he wasted no time on further preliminaries. Framing her face with his palms, he kissed her, his possession as hot and demanding as the primal desire to make this woman his.

And then he did, swallowing her sharp gasp as he lost himself in emotional and physical sensations that made him feel alive and reborn. And in return, he cherished her, and gave her a tenderness he'd forgotten existed.

In the aftermath, with Lauren curled so complacently against his chest, came the knowledge that the woman who'd colored his bleak world with her laughter and spirit and believed in him when he'd thought himself unworthy of such trust and respect would soon be gone.

And he'd be right back where he started.

Alone.

Lauren stood beneath the hot shower spray, trying not to be hurt by the fact that she'd woken up in Rafe's bed alone. After what they'd shared last night, she'd hoped... Oh, Lord, she'd honestly hoped that he'd fall in love with her the way she had with him. His disappearing act this morning didn't bode well for her emotions.

She loved him. The knowledge didn't surprise her. Last night, she'd followed her heart, and it had led her right into Rafe's arms, where she'd known the most glorious pleasure of her life. She'd been the one to make him laugh, but he'd given her a greater joy and fulfillment, the kind of contentment that came with finding the right person.

She'd found the man she wanted to spend the rest of her life with—a stubborn, gorgeous cowboy who wouldn't admit to needing anyone, not even her. He'd made her no promises, and she'd known that before she'd gone to his bed and complicated matters, but that knowledge did nothing to soothe the pain in her heart.

Trying desperately not to dwell on something she didn't have the power to change—mainly Rafe's feelings for her—Lauren finished her shower and dressed in shorts and a blouse. She towel dried her hair, stepped from the hall bathroom into the guest bedroom and found the object of her thoughts sitting on the bed, waiting for her.

Arms braced on his thighs, he watched her with those dark, steel-gray eyes of his. His hair looked as though it had been repeatedly finger combed, shadows underscored his eyes, and a light stubble lined his jaw. She took little gratification in the fact that he looked as miserable as she felt.

"Hi," she said, testing the waters between them, which didn't feel all that calm. There was an underlying tension simmering in the room that made her very uneasy.

He released a long, harsh breath, as if he dreaded what was to come. "I thought we might talk about last night."

His voice was cool, detached, and it made her want to throw something at him, just to rouse a more passionate response from him, even if it was anger. She didn't like that he'd retreated from her, not after how warm and tender he'd been only hours ago.

She crossed to her open suitcase and dropped personal items into the luggage. Then she turned to face him. "Do you regret what happened?" She had to know that much, at least, no matter how painful his answer.

He scrubbed a hand over his jaw, pulling his brows into a deep frown. "No, but it can't happen again."

She crossed her arms, appreciating his honesty but hating his stipulation. "And what if I tell you that I—" At the last second, she refrained from using the word *love,* not certain he was ready to hear her confession. "That I care about you?"

He stood, shaking his head. "It makes no difference how we feel about one another. We don't belong together, Lauren. You have your life in California, with your job and Bright Beginnings, and I've got my ranch here in Wyoming. The two don't mix."

His ruthless argument was sound, but she didn't want to believe that he'd discount what was between them so easily. "How do you know the two *couldn't* mix?" she dared, confronting him head-on.

He accepted her challenge. "Because you're too vibrant to live the rest of your life in a small town and on an isolated ranch." He moved toward her, his gaze softening. When he reached where she stood so defiantly, he touched his fingertips to her cheek, making her unravel and melt. "You're beautiful, and sophisticated, and in time you'd grow bored with a simple cowboy like me." His voice was low and filled with resignation.

She swallowed the huge knot in her throat to hold back an uncharacteristic rush of tears. "Do you really believe I'm that shallow?"

A reluctant smile tugged at his mouth, a little sad and a whole lot tender. "I don't think you're shallow at all. You've got big dreams, Lauren, bigger than the Wyoming sky. I'd only hold you back."

Her chin jutted out. "And what if you're wrong?" she whispered, even as she inwardly admitted that being with Rafe in Cedar Creek would change her whole entire life and certainly redirect her future and dreams.

"I'm not willing to take that chance, for either of our sakes," he said with quiet finality. "Let's just make the best of today and tomorrow—"

"Then go our separate ways?" she snapped, frustration and anger mingling.

"I'm sorry," he said, his eyes flashing a multitude of emotions. "I never meant to hurt you, and you deserve better than what I have to offer." His voice turned gruff, reminding her too much of the brusque, bitter man she'd met weeks ago.

She had a sudden, overwhelming urge to cry, but didn't allow herself that release, not now, and not in front of Rafe. For as much as she'd gotten through to him, she hadn't reached the hardest, most cynical part of his heart. He still believed he wasn't good enough, that he was unworthy of love and acceptance.

If she hadn't proved last night that he was a man to be valued and trusted, then there was little she could do or say to change his opinion of himself.

The sound of a car horn sliced through the tumult of emotions in the room. Rafe stepped back, and the distance, as slight as it was, chilled her.

"That should be Kristin with Chad," he said, his tone flat.

She nodded and turned away from him, needing a few private moments to gather her composure before facing Rafe's sister. "I'll be out in a couple minutes."

After a brief hesitation, he left her room. She listened to his booted steps echo down the hall, then heard him exit the house. And only then did she let the hot, aching tears she'd been holding fall.

Ten minutes later, Lauren walked into the kitchen, forcing a smile for Kristin's benefit. Kristin sat at the table drinking a cup of coffee by herself. After her crying jag, Lauren had scrubbed her face. She knew her eyes were still puffy and her face pale, despite her attempts to add color with a light dusting of makeup. The concern that flitted across Kristin's expression told Lauren her heartache was still apparent.

Crossing to the fresh pot of coffee Kristin must have made, Lauren poured herself a cup, added cream and sugar, and brought it to the table. She slid into the chair next to the other woman, who watched her too closely.

"I brought over some fresh blueberry muffins for breakfast," Kristin said, reaching for a small basket on the table. Opening the cloth napkin, she offered the muffins to Lauren. "Chad helped me make them this morning. I have to admit that he got more batter on his fingers and shirt than he did in the muffin tins."

Lauren laughed, imagining how much fun that had been for Chad. "They look and smell delicious." She didn't have much of an appetite, but Kristin had gone through the trouble of getting them each a small plate and butter from the refrigerator, so she accepted a warm muffin.

Kristin broke open her muffin, and steam rose from the center, testifying to their freshness. "So, did you and Rafe have a nice time last night?"

Lauren nodded as she took a sip of her coffee. "Your brother was actually very friendly with the people at the Elk Lodge, and we had a wonderful time dancing." *In the rain,* she silently added, knowing that impetuous moment and what happened afterward would always remain a personal and private memory, just between her and Rafe.

Kristin slathered butter on her muffin and took a bite, chewing thoughtfully. "If my brother was so congenial last night, then how come he's so grumpy this morning?"

Lauren shrugged, trying her best to appear indifferent when she felt anything but. "I guess he woke up on the wrong side of the bed."

Kristin's brows rose in speculation at Lauren's off-hand comment, but before she could ask more questions Lauren wasn't prepared to answer, Lauren asked, "Where's Chad?"

"He followed Rafe down to the stables."

Worried that Rafe might not be in the frame of mind for a young boy's companionship, she glanced toward the kitchen window. "Maybe I should go get him so Rafe can be alone."

"Don't worry, Rafe was perfectly fine with Chad," Kristin said, waving away her concern. "I've just learned to gauge my brother's moods, and while he was abrupt with me when I asked about last night, he didn't seem to mind Chad's company.''

"Good,'' Lauren said, relieved. She took a bite of her melt-in-your-mouth muffin, then another, surprised to find that she was hungry, after all.

Kristin watched her over the rim of her mug. "You know, this may be none of my business, but is there something going on between you and my brother?''

The cakey confection stuck in Lauren's throat, and she forced it down with a deliberate swallow. "Uh, like what?''

"Maybe something romantic.'' There was a wistful note in Kristin's voice that conveyed her hope to see Rafe happy. "I know he was a grouch this morning, and I don't want to pry into the reasons why, but I've seen a big difference in Rafe this past week. I've caught him looking at you a few times in a way I've never seen him look at another woman, and there just seems to be a spark between you two.'' She smiled impishly, her green eyes soft. "I thought, well, maybe if you two had a little time alone together, like last night, something magical would happen.''

Oh, something magical and wonderful had happened, all right. Lauren had fallen deeply, irrevocably in love. Except Rafe was denying his emotions and the intimate connection between them.

Lauren attempted to explain her relationship with Rafe to Kristin, choosing her words carefully. "I care about Rafe, very much, but there's nothing I can do when he won't accept what I openly offer him. He has a hard time believing he's a good, decent man.''

"Yeah, that's Rafe, all right, blaming himself for something that's not his fault." Kristin shook her head, sadness dimming her gaze. "After my mother passed away he was torn between being responsible for me and trying to please my father, who expected way too much from Rafe. Somewhere along the way, he lost sight of what was important to *him*. And then the accident with Keith and being hailed a hero when he believed he was responsible for what happened just shut him down emotionally."

"I know," she admitted quietly, picking at the muffin crumbs on her plate. "He told me everything, but until he quits condemning himself for what happened in the past, there's no way he'll allow himself any other future than what he has here, alone on this ranch."

Kristin released a long, burdensome sigh. "I guess that's something he's just going to have to figure out for himself. The hard way."

Unfortunately, Lauren agreed, though that acceptance only added to the grief she was experiencing. Shaking off her melancholy mood and the depressing thought of leaving Rafe, she reached for another muffin and buttered it.

"Lauren?"

Kristin's soft, tentative voice captured Lauren's attention. Mouth full of muffin, she glanced up, surprised to see a glimmer of nervousness in the other woman's eyes. "Yes?"

Kristin absently ran a finger along the rim of her coffee mug. "I'd, um, like to talk to you about Chad."

A belated thought occurred to Lauren as she finished her breakfast. "He wasn't a problem last night, was he?"

A beatific smile claimed Kristin's lips. "Oh, no, he was a complete joy," she assured Lauren. "We've really enjoyed being around him this past week."

"I'm glad." Lauren knew the feeling was mutual. The boy had spent as much time with Kristin and James as he had with Rafe and talked about all three of them with enthusiasm and affection. "You all have made his wish something he'll always remember and cherish. Thank you for that."

"I should be thanking you," Kristin said sincerely.

Her gratitude perplexed Lauren. "Oh?"

Kristin nodded, and appearing anxious once again, she stood and took their empty plates to the sink. Lauren waited patiently while she rinsed the dishes, feeling as though the other woman had more to say and was trying to gather the fortitude to do it.

Kristin turned to face Lauren, bracing her hands on the counter behind her. "After Chad fell asleep last night, James and I started talking about the possibility of adopting a child."

Lauren remembered Kristin's uncertainty when they'd talked about adoption, and her chest swelled with optimism for the young couple. "Kristin, that's wonderful."

Kristin twisted her hands together at her waist, and she blurted, "We'd like to know what our chances would be of adopting Chad."

Lauren was speechless for a moment. "But I thought—"

"I know I told you I wanted a baby," Kristin interrupted in a rush. "But after being with Chad this past week, having an infant no longer matters. We adore Chad, he fits in our lives perfectly, and if it's at all possible we want to give him a stable home with two loving parents."

"I'd like that, too," Lauren whispered, her throat tight with tears of happiness for a little boy who'd lost so much yet was being granted a bright beginning of his own. Standing, Lauren crossed the kitchen to Kristin and grabbed her hand, giving it a reassuring squeeze. "You and James would make wonderful parents."

Kristin released a shaky breath, new worries springing to life in her gaze. "Could you help us do that?"

Lauren smiled, knowing she'd make Chad's case a priority when she returned to California. "Yeah, I think I can."

Kristin hugged Lauren in a warm, heartfelt embrace. "Thank you."

Once the emotional moment passed, Lauren told Kristin the standard procedure. "I have to take him back to California with me tomorrow, and it'll take a few weeks to get a court order approved for temporary custody so he can live here with you and James until adoption proceedings are finalized."

"Whatever it takes, we want Chad," Kristin affirmed, without a trace of doubt or hesitation, and with enough love to encompass a little boy who'd made an indelible mark on their lives.

Lauren wished she'd been as lucky with Rafe.

CHAPTER NINE

LAUREN stepped into the paddock where Rafe was saddling the third of three mares. His back was to her as he worked, and the muscles across his shoulders bunched beneath the cotton shirt he wore as he looped the girth into a tie knot. His head was bent as he murmured soothing words to the animal and ran a broad hand down the mare's sleek neck.

Lauren remembered those hands on her bare skin last night, and Rafe's deep, gentle voice whispering in her ear, and her entire body tingled. How was she supposed to go back to a life without Rafe in it when he'd shown her what love was all about—physically and emotionally?

The mare caught sight of her, and as if in greeting, the big chestnut nodded at Lauren and blew out a soft snort of breath. Rafe turned, and though his expression remained impassive beneath the brim of his Stetson, his gaze roamed hot and hungry down the length of her. Her pulse kicked up in tempo, and heat suffused her veins.

Ignoring her body's automatic response to this earthy, sensual man, she smiled, determined to make the best of what little time they had together. "Chad said you wanted to see me, and to make sure I was wearing my hat." She tipped the Stetson he'd given her. "What's up?"

He returned his attention to the horse. "I thought we could take Chad out for one last ride this afternoon, since you'll be leaving for the airport by eleven tomorrow morning.''

His civil and polite tone grated on her nerves, especially after the intimacies they'd shared. She kept her frustrations locked away and struggled to maintain an upbeat attitude. ''I'd like that.''

He was quiet for a moment as he adjusted the stirrups, then finally said, ''My sister told me about her and James possibly adopting Chad.''

Nodding, she tucked her hands into the back pockets of the jeans she'd changed into. ''I'm going to do everything I can to see that it happens.''

''Good.'' His stormy gray eyes met hers, the depths filled with gratitude and a rare warmth. ''They deserve to be happy.''

''Yeah, they do,'' she agreed, smiling softly. ''And Chad is a great kid.''

He stared at her for a long, silent second, a flicker of tenderness and regret brushing across his features. She waited, holding her breath, hoping for the impossible—that Rafe would realize he deserved to be happy, too. With her. Instead, he gave his head a fierce shake, as if to dislodge the fanciful notion, and finished readying the horses.

Half an hour later the three of them were riding in a stretch of green pasture dotted with a few hedges and lined with trees. Chad took the lead, spurring his mare into a strong, fast gallop, leaving Rafe and Lauren in the rear.

Rafe slowed his horse to an easy walk, and Lauren followed suit beside him, allowing Chad the freedom to enjoy the wide open space as long as he stayed within sight. Lauren wanted to be near Rafe even if the time they spent in each other's company was quiet and charged with undercurrents of desire and longing Rafe refused to acknowledge.

The silence didn't last long. Rafe glanced her way, his expression annoyed, his palm absently rubbing his scarred thigh. "You don't have to stay behind with me."

Refusing to let his brusque attitude bother her—not on their last day together—she flashed him a sassy grin. "And you don't have to be such a grouch."

The corner of his mouth twitched, and he averted his gaze without further comment.

"Is your leg bothering you much?" She asked the question conversationally, though she knew his injured thigh was the reason he was taking the ride easy.

"I'll be fine." As if to prove as much, he spurred his horse into a canter and made his way across the wide pasture toward Chad.

Lauren shook her head ruefully, certain Rafe's leg would ache later from the vigorous exercise. She thought about joining the duo, but decided against infringing on their last ride together. Remaining at a discreet distance, enjoying the clean breeze blowing through her hair, Lauren imprinted everything about Wyoming, and the man she'd fallen in love with, to memory.

Rafe and Chad raced across the pasture, Chad exhibiting a competitive streak that seemed to impress Rafe, if Rafe's complimentary comments about Chad's riding abilities were any indication. The boy glowed from his praise and continually looked Lauren's way to seek her approval, too. She encouraged him with lots of grins while applauding and cheering his efforts. The afternoon was fun. The more skill and endurance Chad displayed, the more Rafe coaxed him and his horse to perform challenging maneuvers.

After a while, Rafe rode to where Lauren had been watching them from the cool shelter of a large shade tree and brought his horse to a stop a few feet from hers. The faint lines bracketing his eyes and creasing his brow, the way his right hand pressed against his thigh, testified to the discomfort he was experiencing.

"Are you quitting already?" Chad asked, the disappointment in his tone evident.

"Just taking a break." Rafe grimaced as he shifted in his saddle to find a more comfortable position. "Why don't you try jumping over that low hedge over there?" he suggested, to keep Chad occupied while he gave his leg a rest.

Chad eyed the two-foot hedge, chewing on his bottom lip uncertainly. "I've never jumped before."

"There's a first time for everything, cowboy," Rafe prompted in an attempt to dismiss the boy's fears. "Just keep your body in rhythm with the horse, and she'll do the work for you. Go on and give it a try."

"All right." Hesitation touched Chad's voice, but he circled with his mare, giving himself plenty of distance to gain the momentum they needed to vault the obstacle. Then he raced his chestnut toward the shrub, his youthful features set in determination.

"Yeah, that's it," Rafe prompted from the sidelines as they watched horse and rider glide smoothly across the flat meadow. "Urge her faster."

And Chad did, leaning into the horse, his little body moving fluidly with the strong, powerful mare

beneath him. Lauren's heart picked up in anticipation
of the brave feat Chad would perform.

"The boy is a natural," Rafe said in appreciation
as Chad and the horse catapulted over the hedge.

The actual jump was perfection, causing Lauren's
breath to catch in awe, but the landing lacked stability. The horse's left hoof touched down on an un-
even patch of ground, and the mare stumbled. The
rough, jerking motion unseated Chad. The boy sailed
over the horse's head.

Chad's airborne cry of terror ripped through
Lauren, and she watched in paralyzed fear as the boy
landed in a twisted heap on the ground. *"No!"* she
screamed, as if the one word had the power to stop
the horrific scene unfolding in front of them.

Rafe released a vicious curse and immediately
spurred his horse toward Chad's lifeless form, un-
mindful of the wind stealing the Stetson from his
head. He jumped off his mare before the animal
stopped and dropped to his knees by the boy's side,
his hands moving gently over Chad's body as he
checked for injuries.

Lauren knelt next to Rafe but didn't get in his way
while he continued to examine Chad. Panic filled her
at the sight of Chad's pale face, the slow rise and
fall of his chest as he breathed. At least he *was*
breathing, she thought gratefully.

"Come on, Chad," Rafe whispered urgently, desperately, as his fingers tenderly probed the boy's
chest, checking for any broken ribs. Seemingly satisfied that all was well there, he moved on, assessing
hips and legs. "Talk to me, son."

Chad rolled his head toward the sound of Rafe's
voice, an anguished moan escaping his lips. His

lashes fluttered open, and he grimaced in obvious pain. "My arm," he croaked, then winced when he tried to lift the limb toward Rafe. "It hurts really bad."

"Okay, cowboy, don't try and move," Rafe said in a low, soothing tone that contradicted the fear etched on his features. "Lie still while I check your arm."

Lauren glided her fingertips along Chad's cheek, offering him comfort, trying to distract him while Rafe investigated his injury.

Chad stared at her, his eyes lacking their normal sparkle. "I almost did it," he said, disappointment creasing his brow.

"You were great," she assured him with a smile. "It was the horse that messed up."

"Next time I'm gonna make it over that hedge without falling," he said, then sucked in a breath as Rafe touched a particularly tender spot.

"There won't be a next time," Rafe interjected harshly, his voice infused with sharp finality. He glanced her way, his lips flattening into a grim line.

Worry made her pulse speed up. "What is it?"

"I think his arm is fractured." He clawed a hand through his hair, looking haggard and emotionally anguished. "We've got to get him to the doctor."

Three long hours later, Lauren and Rafe returned from Dr. Kendal's office with Chad. The boy's left arm was encased in a cast from wrist to elbow. An X ray showed that Chad had fractured the middle of his forearm. Other than a few bumps and bruises from his tumble off the horse, the doctor had diagnosed him as extremely resilient and in good physical condition.

Rafe said little on the drive home, though Lauren knew guilt was eating him up. It was nothing he'd said at the doctor's office, but his eyes spoke volumes, as did the clenching of his firm, chiseled jaw. Lauren ached to reassure Rafe, to do or say something to erase the dark shadows lining his features, but knew this wasn't the time or the place to bring up a subject that would no doubt turn into an argument.

Lauren had called Kristin and James from the doctor's office. They were waiting on the front porch when they arrived home. Kristin rushed down the steps with James following, and as soon as Chad exited the vehicle, Kristin began fussing over him.

"Oh, honey," she crooned sympathetically as her fingers brushed a lock of hair off his brow, her maternal instincts as natural and real as the fondness shining in her eyes for Chad. "Are you in much pain?"

Chad's mouth turned up in a sheepish smile, though he didn't seem to mind Kristin's attention or affection. "It hurts just a little."

"Well, let's get you into the house and make you comfortable." Kristin guided him gently toward the screen door, careful not to jostle his cast. "How about something cool to drink? And maybe a cookie or two?"

Chad nodded enthusiastically. "Yes, please."

James stayed behind, concern evident in his gaze as he glanced from Rafe to Lauren. "Is everything really okay with Chad?"

Rafe said nothing and looked away.

"He'll be sore from the fall, but Dr. Kendal assured us he'll be fine." Lauren followed James up the porch steps. "No permanent damage was done."

James reached for the door handle but didn't open the door. The smile on his face was full of gratitude and warmth. "I know he's not ours yet, but Kristin and I can't help but worry about him."

The man's words touched Lauren's heart, making her anxious to reunite Chad with these two people who would love him unconditionally. "Worrying is what parents are supposed to do."

"Yeah," James agreed, nodding. "And I suppose this won't be the last time a horse throws him. I've had my share of falls."

Lauren glanced at Rafe, who stood by the porch railing, staring out at the ranch. She'd expected him to agree with James's comment, but his expression was shuttered, and he looked in no mood to contribute anything positive to the conversation.

"Why don't you go on in and talk to Chad?" Lauren suggested, wanting to be alone with Rafe so she could talk to him privately. "I'm sure he's eager to share the whole exciting story with you and Kristin. Rafe and I will be along in a few minutes."

James looked from her to Rafe and nodded. She waited until James disappeared inside, then crossed the porch to stand in front of the man she was beginning to understand all too well.

She regarded him intently, and spoke the words she'd been wanting to express since Chad's fall. "It wasn't your fault, you know."

"The hell it wasn't!" His tone was low and heated, fueling the personal anguish Lauren detected in his eyes. "You would have thought I'd learned from my actions with Keith, but I'm just as aggressive and self-centered as my old man.''

"That's not true," she argued vehemently.

"Isn't it?" he asked, fury and frustration darkening his gaze to a violent shade of gray.

Tension swirled between them, but she wasn't at all intimidated by his escalating temper. "It was an accident, Rafe."

"Which never would have happened if I hadn't pushed him to jump over that hedge!" He jabbed an angry finger toward the house and the boy inside. "He wasn't ready to jump yet. I kept urging him to do it. I could have *killed* him!"

Rafe's guilt was a tangible thing, cloaking her in the raw emotion radiating from him. A cold, hard knot formed in her stomach, and she tried to reach beyond the torment gripping him. "You had nothing to do with it. The horse stumbled, and Chad lost his balance."

He impaled her with his steady, heated gaze. "I had everything to do with Chad's fall. If I hadn't been so aggressive and irresponsible—"

"Rafe?"

Lauren and Rafe spun around at the sound of Chad's voice. The boy stood on the other side of the screen door, his eyes filled with distress. Kristin came up behind Chad and gently rested her hands on his shoulders in silent support.

Chad swallowed and shifted uneasily, obviously uncomfortable now that everyone's attention was directed at him. "At first I was scared to jump over that hedge," he admitted, his voice faltering. "But I did it because I really wanted to, not because you told me to, Rafe."

Rafe turned his head and squeezed his eyes shut, as if he couldn't believe Chad.

"It was *my* choice to make that jump," Chad went on, his quivering chin lifting courageously. "And no one is to blame for what happened to me. Lauren is right. My fall was an accident."

Lauren waited for Chad's heartfelt words to take effect on Rafe, hoping he'd realize the past had nothing to do with what happened today. Hoping, too, that he'd finally accept that he was nothing like his father, that he was an honorable man who'd never deliberately hurt anyone, especially a young boy.

Rafe looked from Chad to Lauren, uncertainty flickering in the depths of his eyes along with the need to believe Chad's words—to believe in himself. Lauren watched him waver, but in the end something held him back.

With a low, frustrated sound, he scrubbed a hand down his face, and turned and left the porch.

Lauren folded a pair of jeans and put them into the open suitcase on the bed she'd slept in for the past week. Another hour and she and Chad would be on their way to the airport.

At least Chad would be returning, Lauren thought with some optimism, truly happy that his Bright Beginnings wish would evolve into a dream come true. Chad deserved to be part of a loving family, and Lauren couldn't ask for more adoring parents than Kristin and James.

Hiding a yawn behind her hand, Lauren continued packing, her mind on one final task before she and Chad left Cedar Creek. A mission that would foretell her future.

She'd spent a restless night tossing and turning, trying to figure out what she was going to do about her feelings for a certain grouchy, grumpy bull-riding champion. She'd never expected to fall in love on her week-long vacation in Wyoming, yet there was no denying she'd gone and done just that. Her mother would no doubt be appalled to learn her only daughter had given her heart to a cowboy who raised Quarter Horses instead of to one of the doctors or lawyers she'd set Lauren up with. But Lauren didn't care about social status. All those men had left her cold, and treated Bright Beginnings as a hobby.

She had Rafe's respect. Now she wanted his love.

Rafe had told her the two of them didn't belong together, that her life in California and her dedication to Bright Beginnings didn't mix with his simple lifestyle. But she'd discovered there was something greater and far more important here in Cedar Creek, and she couldn't ignore the undeniable pull on her heart. She'd found the love she'd been searching for, the fairy tale, and it all began and ended with Rafe.

She closed her suitcase and zipped it up, silently admitting that Rafe wasn't an easy man to love. But despite his gruffness and aloof attitude, she knew he had feelings for her, too. The night they'd made love showed her another side to the man, giving her a glimpse of tenderness, laughter and exciting male possession.

She yearned for that man, and more.

She checked on Chad, who was in the kitchen eating pancakes with Kristin and James. They'd arrived early that morning to spend time with the boy, and as difficult as she knew it was for Kristin and James to see Chad leave, they were at least comforted in the knowledge that there would be a reunion, and soon.

There was only one thing left for Lauren to do—risk her heart, and hope her love made the difference with Rafe.

"You've been down here all morning. Were you even going to say goodbye?"

The sound of Lauren's soft, sweet voice washed over Rafe, and he turned from where he'd been standing at the end of the stable corridor, staring at the horses grazing in the pasture. His morning chores had long since been done, and he'd spent the last hour debating whether or not to return to the main house to be with Chad and Lauren before they headed off to the airport. Knowing Kristin and James were spending every moment available with Chad, Rafe had thought it best to make himself scarce.

It had been a convenient excuse, but the truth was tangled in his feelings for this woman in front of him. He'd yet to sort his emotions into a semblance of coherence. He tried not to be affected by the glimmer of tenderness in her gaze, but he was merely a mortal man and couldn't help but ache for what could never be his—this incredible, unselfish woman.

Clearing his throat, he asked, "Is it time for you and Chad to leave?"

"Soon." She slowly moved closer, the skirt of her summer dress swirling around her long, slender legs. "I wanted to thank you for granting Chad's wish and for being his hero. Your generosity has changed his life for the better."

He didn't want Lauren's gratitude. He wanted—hell, he didn't know what he wanted anymore. He felt confused and irritable, and longed for things he had no business wanting in his isolated life. The thought mocked him, because he knew after experiencing Lauren's smiles and laughter, living in the solitary world he'd created for himself would no longer appeal to him.

Yet he was convinced she didn't belong here, not in Cedar Creek and not with him. Not when she had so much to offer the foster children she worked with. Not when her wealthy parents expected a more suitable match for their only daughter.

Lauren drew a deep breath, her gaze holding his steadily. "Before I leave, there's something I need to tell you."

He kept his expression carefully shuttered and thrust his hands into the front pockets of his jeans. "And what's that?"

A smile trembled on her lips, and a wealth of emotion brimmed in her eyes. "I love you," she said simply.

Rafe reeled from her declaration, her words momentarily rendering him speechless. Shock eventually gave way to denial, and he scowled at her in an attempt to put everything into perspective. "You can't love me."

"Why not?" Her tone held a trace of humor, though there was nothing amusing about the situation. Closing the distance between them, she pressed a hand to his chest, right over his frantically beating heart. "Because you think you're unlovable?"

He grasped her wrist but couldn't bear to push her hand away. Her touch warmed him deep inside, where he was so cold and miserable. "Lauren..." Her name escaped him on a gruff warning.

She ignored it, stepping closer, surrounding him in her light, feminine scent. "You only have to ask me to stay here with you, and I would."

He groaned, the sound rife with despair. "That's impossible, and we both know it."

She tilted her head, a smile touching the corners of her mouth. "Why is it so impossible?"

"Because you have Bright Beginnings, and I would only hold you back," he said. "I'd never ask you to give up your work."

"Who says I have to? The wonderful thing about Bright Beginnings is that I can run the foundation from anywhere." Her hand fell away, and she released a soft sigh. "I've thought about this all night long, Rafe, and I'm willing to work with foster agencies in the neighboring cities so I can be with you."

So I can be with you. He swallowed hard, overwhelmed that she was willing to sacrifice so much for him and at the same time offer him her complete faith and trust. Yet he couldn't ignore the doubts swamping him. He knew she deserved far better than the man he was. He put his blackest reputation straight on the line to save her from future heartache.

"You think you're in love with me, but I'm not looking for a wife, and I have no plans to ever have a family of my own. I think I've proved by my actions yesterday with Chad that I've inherited my father's harsher, more aggressive tendencies."

"The only thing you're guilty of is believing you could ever hurt a child or another person," Lauren argued. "What happened with Keith was an unfortunate accident. Same with Chad. You're nothing like your father, Rafe."

"Yeah, well, I'm not willing to risk a child's emotional welfare to find out.'' Jamming his hands on his hips, he summoned the will to say the words that would banish this woman from his life but not from his heart. ''I don't want you here, Lauren,'' he said bluntly, the lie ripping through him like a knife.

Moisture welled in her blue eyes, and then she lifted that stubborn chin of hers. ''What we shared the other night, it meant nothing to you?''

He couldn't bring himself to say the word no, so he shook his head and forced out, ''I'm sorry.'' *For hurting you, and loving you when I have no right to.*

''Damn you, Rafe,'' she said, her voice filled with frustration. Then determination sparked in her gaze, and she advanced on him. Before he could guess what she intended, she'd wrapped her arms around his neck and pulled his mouth to hers.

His entire body stiffened, and his hands shot out and grabbed her hips in an attempt to stop her sensual assault. She clung to him, her warm, sweet lips sliding over his, parting them for a deeper kiss. Unable to resist her, he gave himself over to their final embrace, taking greedily what she offered, needing this one last kiss to carry him through a lifetime.

Too soon, she pulled back, and he let her go.

''I don't believe you, Rafe,'' she whispered, staring at him, hope etching her features. ''But I'll leave, if that's what you really want.''

''It is,'' he managed, steeling himself against the hurt glimmering in her eyes. He hated himself for inflicting such misery on this woman he'd fallen in love with but would never take as his own. He had nothing substantial to offer her.

''I'm no hero, Lauren,'' he said gruffly, curling

his hands into fists at his sides to keep from touching her one last time. "I told you that from the beginning, and that fact still remains. Go home to California, where you belong."

CHAPTER TEN

SITTING across from her mother at the outdoor café where they were having lunch, Lauren half-listened to Maureen as she talked about a recent party she'd attended, about how Lauren had missed a wonderful opportunity to meet a few eligible men. Unfortunately, Lauren wasn't interested—she'd left her heart in Wyoming, given to an obstinate man who refused to accept her love and unconditional faith in him.

She'd foolishly harbored the hope that Rafe would come to his senses and realize he loved her, too, yet for the past month the only people in Wyoming she'd had any contact with were Kristin and James. Chad's case was progressing without any problems. Lauren kept her conversations with Kristin focused on business, refusing to involve Kristin in her feelings for Rafe.

She was scheduled to return to Cedar Creek in another week, to take Chad to his new family, a brief, formal trip that would be as wonderful for Chad as it would be painful for her. She only planned to be there for the weekend to help Chad settle in, yet she fully expected to see Rafe. No doubt he'd be formal and polite. Their awkward encounter was something she wasn't looking forward to enduring.

"You haven't been the same since you returned from your trip to Wyoming," Maureen Richmond commented, pulling Lauren from her thoughts. "Are you feeling okay?"

Stabbing her fork into her chicken Caesar salad, Lauren summoned a smile. "I'm fine, just busy at work." Which had been her own choice. The more absorbed she kept herself with her foster cases, the less time she had to think about Rafe. Unfortunately, there was no escaping thoughts of him when she crawled into bed and remembered the warmth and gentleness of his touch. No, those were memories that would haunt her for years to come.

"Maybe you should take some time off from the agency," Maureen suggested, her pale blue eyes expressing concern. "You work too much, at Blair and with Bright Beginnings. Dealing with all those cases must be emotionally draining."

Catching the barest hint of disapproval in her mother's tone, Lauren sighed and took a long drink of her iced tea. She wished Maureen would offer more support.

"I enjoy my work," Lauren stated firmly, hating that she had to defend something so important to her.

Maureen dabbed her lips with her napkin, nodding absently. "Well, I think I might have someone who might cheer you up and take your mind off of work."

Unless her mother had managed to locate Rafe and change his mind about her, Lauren seriously doubted her claim. "Mom, I'm really not interested."

Maureen waved a manicured hand in the air, ignoring Lauren's refusal to be set up with an eligible, suitable male. "Do you remember Vivian Wingate, the interior decorator who helped me redesign the living room?"

Lauren didn't, and though she shook her head, her mother continued, excitement shining in her eyes.

"Well, I found out her son, Robert, is an established pediatrician, and we both thought the two of you would get along wonderfully."

Lauren raised a brow. "Really?" She didn't bother disguising the skepticism in her voice. Rarely did she "get along wonderfully" with the men her mother chose for her to date. Most were arrogant and were looking for a dutiful wife to adorn their arm.

"I saw a picture of him, and he's very handsome, too." Maureen beamed, as if proud of the most recent, good-looking, wealthy suitor she'd discovered for Lauren.

Tired of her mother's matchmaking and knowing there was only one way to stop it, she said calmly, "I'm sure Robert is very attractive and quite a catch, but I'm in love with someone else."

Her mother blinked at her, momentarily stunned by her confession. Then she frowned in bewilderment. "I didn't realize you were seeing someone seriously."

Lauren set her fork next to her plate. Now that she'd revealed her feelings for Rafe to her mother, she decided she might as well tell her everything. "It happened quite unexpectedly, actually. His name is Rafe Dalton. He's the man I met in Wyoming, the one that granted Chad Evans his wish."

Maureen's mouth pursed in disapproval. "The one that rides bulls for a living?"

She hadn't thought her mother had been listening when she'd vented her frustration over trying to contact Rafe and him ignoring her letters. A grin quirked Lauren's mouth. Leave it to her mother to remember

Rafe's occupation. "Rafe used to be a bull rider," she clarified. "But now he raises Quarter Horses on his ranch."

Pushing her half-eaten quiche to the side, Maureen grew unusually quiet as she searched Lauren's expression. After a long moment passed, she asked, "And you really love him?"

"Yes, I do." Lauren couldn't deny what was in her heart.

She expected censure from her mother for falling for a cowboy. But Maureen's gaze softened with a rare understanding, and resignation, too. "And how does he feel about you?"

Smiling sadly, Lauren swirled her straw in her drink. "I know he cares about me, possibly even loves me, but he's too stubborn to admit it." It felt peculiar discussing such an intimate, private topic with her mother, who'd spent so many years foisting prospective beaus upon her. But she appreciated the listening ear. "He doesn't think we belong together."

"And you do?"

"I could make it work if he was willing to meet me halfway." She drew a deep breath and admitted her deepest feelings. "He's everything I've ever wanted in a man. Rafe is warm, and sensitive, and fun, even if he won't admit to those traits. And he respects *me*, and what I do with Bright Beginnings."

A seldom-seen tenderness shone in Maureen's gaze. "You really do love him."

Lauren's throat grew tight with so many different sentiments. Most predominant was the feeling that her love hadn't been able to heal Rafe's emotional scars. "Yeah, I really do."

Silence settled between them as their waitress cleared their lunch plates and refilled their glasses of iced tea. Lauren thought their conversation was over until her mother reached across the table and grasped her hand, capturing Lauren's attention.

"I want to tell you something," Maureen began softly, her fingers trembling slightly against Lauren's hand. "Before I met your father, I was seeing a young man your grandfather didn't approve of. His name was Michael, and he was a waiter at the country club we belonged to. After a few months of sneaking around and dating, we fell in love. We talked about running off and getting married, but when my father heard about our plans to elope, he ended the relationship, furious that I'd marry such a common, ordinary man. And because I was so young and naive and didn't know any better, I obeyed my father."

Lauren stared at her mother in stunned silence, unable to believe she'd stowed away such a scandalous secret.

"Don't look so surprised," Maureen muttered, her face flushing. "I met your father about a year after that, and we married for, well, more necessary reasons."

Lauren nodded.

"I've always regretted letting Michael go, and that I didn't fight for *us*." Melancholy tinged Maureen's voice, and sorrow filled her blue eyes. "He might not have been wealthy or prominent enough for my father, but I loved him more than I've loved any other man."

Confusion creased Lauren's brow as she digested her mother's astonishing story. "But I thought you wanted me to marry someone upstanding and affluent."

"Oh, I do," she admitted, unabashed. "I know I haven't set the greatest example, but I was hoping you'd fall in love with one of the men I set you up with. But I of all people know that you can't necessarily pick the person you're going to fall in love with. Sometimes, it just happens. And when it does, you should follow your heart."

"To Wyoming?" Lauren wanted her mother's approval and needed to know that in this one endeavor, she had her support.

Maureen shrugged, moisture sheening her eyes. "Your happiness is what matters most to me, whether it be here in California or in Wyoming with the man you love."

Lauren felt a warm glow of acceptance spread through her. In that priceless moment, mother and daughter shared a mutual respect and admiration that paved the way for the kind of special, close relationship Lauren had always wanted.

Rafe opened the screen door for his sister to enter his house, eyeing the casserole dish she carried. A delicious scent filled his senses, and he recognized the aroma—tender pot roast and potatoes.

While he appreciated Kristin's cooking skills and her leftovers, he knew they were an excuse for her to stop by and make sure he was doing okay. He'd never admit it, but he looked forward to Kristin's company and her visits. After experiencing Lauren's bright personality and sassy conversation, he no longer craved solitude.

That particular revelation was one he was still trying to come to accept.

The past few weeks had been hell. As hard as he tried to forget about Lauren and the impact she'd made on his life in the short time she'd been in Cedar Creek, nothing banished her from his mind. One week, and she'd made an indelible impression, on him and the town. As much as he told himself he'd done the right thing, the honorable thing, by sending her back to California, he couldn't convince his heart of the noble deed. He hoped, in time, that the misery of missing Lauren would fade. The despair of loving her was something he suspected would take an eternity to ease.

Taking the meal from Kristin, he headed for the kitchen with her following. "If you've come to check up on me, I'm just fine." The gruffness in his tone was all growl, and no bite.

"And just as ornery as ever, I see," she commented wryly. "After this week, you won't have to put up with me as often. I'm going to be too busy to worry about feeding you."

Setting the casserole dish on the counter, he turned to face his sister, unable to miss the bright excitement sparkling in her green eyes. "Oh?"

"Yeah." A jubilant smile spread across her face, and she clasped her hands in front of her as if to contain the elation bubbling to the surface. "Temporary guardianship for Chad has been granted until the adoption is finalized. He'll be coming home next Saturday."

Rafe smiled, genuinely pleased that his sister and James would finally have the family they'd always wanted. Folding her into his embrace, he gave her a hug to congratulate her and to express his happiness. "That's wonderful, Sis."

Kristin glanced at him, surprise widening her eyes. "Wow, giving you the news was worth seeing you smile."

"You weren't supposed to see that." He scowled at her, and she laughed.

"James and I are planning a welcome-home party for Chad on Sunday," she went on enthusiastically. "And as his new uncle, I fully expect you to attend."

He had to admit that being an uncle had a nice ring to it. "I wouldn't miss it for anything."

"Good." Kristin grew serious and touched him gently on the cheek. "If it wasn't for you, none of this would be possible. I have you to thank for bringing Chad into our lives and giving me and James a gift more precious than gold. Because of you, we're going to have a family."

Rafe felt humbled by his sister's words. "I had nothing to do with it."

"How can you say that?" She frowned at him. "You granted Chad's wish."

Finding it difficult to accept his sister's praise, he propped his hands on his hips and grasped for levity. "If I remember correctly, I was *coerced*."

"Do you regret it?" she asked softly.

Her question reached straight to his heart, giving him a moment's pause. How could he regret bringing Chad into Kristin's life and granting his sister *her* fondest wish? "No, I don't."

"I'm glad," she whispered, her voice emotion-filled. "You were Chad's hero, but now you're my personal hero."

Rafe's belly clenched, and he automatically rejected the title that had brought him nothing but grief. "I'm nobody's hero, Kristin."

"That's where you're wrong, Rafe," Kristin answered, a smile curving her mouth. "You're a man with integrity and courage and the ability to care and give. You showed me that, and more, when Mom died, and every day since. Even if you don't want to admit to those caring qualities, I see them all the time."

He blew out a harsh breath that did nothing to ease the tension twisting within him. "Don't make me out to be something I'm not. Past actions prove I'm too much like our father."

She scoffed at that. "Heroes come in many forms, Rafe, but all require a chivalrous heart. That's something our father *never* had." She let that statement sink in before continuing. "You and Lauren have those generous traits in common, and it would be a shame if you let such a wonderful woman slip away."

Rafe glanced away from his sister's steady gaze, unable to argue with her, not when Kristin's words held too much truth.

He heard her sigh. Then her footsteps started toward the living room. Before she left, she stopped and asked, "Did I mention that Lauren would be the one bringing Chad on Saturday?"

A sound between humor and hopelessness escaped him. Seeing Lauren again would be one of the most difficult things he'd ever have to endure. No, he silently amended, watching her leave—*again*—would be pure torture. "No, you didn't."

"Just in case you're wondering, she'll be staying

with us for the weekend, then returning to California on Monday.''

Rafe hung his head and listened to Kristin leave the house, her words playing havoc with his emotions. He spent the evening thinking about everything his sister had said, arguing with himself over all the reasons he didn't deserve a woman like Lauren or her healing faith and love. She'd given him the laughter, warmth and tenderness missing from his life and was willing to sacrifice so much to be with him. In return, he'd been incredibly selfish, allowing his fears to push her away when she was the one person besides his sister who believed in him.

That was the ultimate reason to fight for the incredible, stubborn, sassy woman.

He wanted to be Lauren's hero in every way that mattered—which gave him a week to straighten up his attitude and figure out a way to prove that he wanted and needed her in his life.

Forever.

She and Chad had been at Kristin and James's for over twenty-four hours, and Lauren had yet to see Rafe. She put on a happy facade to greet the steady stream of people arriving for the welcome-home party being held in Chad's honor, but deep inside she couldn't ignore the hurt and disappointment curling through her. She'd arrived in Wyoming yesterday with high hopes that Rafe would make an attempt at reconciliation. All she wanted was half an effort on his part, something to indicate he cared about her even a little, and she'd do the rest.

She resigned herself to the fact that he'd meant

what he'd said a month ago—he didn't want her here, and she didn't belong.

Watching as Chad played ball with Randy and a few other boys, Lauren smiled and mingled with the townsfolk, accepting their gracious comments about Bright Beginnings and trying to keep her thoughts from wandering to Chad's one missing guest. Kristin had briefly mentioned that Rafe planned to stop by, but as the afternoon wore on, Lauren began to doubt the other woman's claim.

"I don't think I've ever seen a happier kid," a familiar male voice said. Jason sat next to her at one of the picnic tables set up in the yard. "You've got to feel damn good about what you do."

Lauren met Jason's warm, friendly gaze, and smiled. "I have to confess that granting wishes does make me feel like a fairy godmother with a magic wand. Especially when one of my clients lives happily every after."

Jason picked up the hamburger on his plate and grinned at her, his eyebrows bobbing. "Ah, another fairy tale with a satisfying ending."

Unlike her fairy tale with Rafe, which had ended too abruptly. Pushing potato salad around on her plate, she tilted her head and regarded Jason teasingly. "You looking for another article for the Cedar Creek *Gazette*?"

He shrugged as he chewed a bite of burger. "I do plan to put Chad and his new family on Monday's front page, but that's not why I'm here."

Curiosity got the best of her. "Then why are you here?"

"The same reason everyone else is, to welcome Chad to Cedar Creek." His gaze encompassed the front lawn and the few dozen people who'd come to support Kristin and James in this very important endeavor in their lives. "He'll never lack for acceptance here."

Lauren's heart warmed, and her throat grew tight with emotion. There was no doubt Chad would be well loved. "I'm glad to hear that."

Jason took a swallow of soda, his gaze taking on a mischievous sparkle. "And I do believe there's a bigger story to cover here at the party, with your permission, of course."

That caught her attention. His request totally perplexed her. "Excuse me?"

"Have you seen what Rafe has done to his place?" he asked off-handedly, then crunched into a potato chip.

"No." Kristin and James had picked her and Chad up from the airport yesterday and driven straight to their place. Lauren couldn't imagine what kind of change to Rafe's spread would make Jason look so anxious. "Actually, I haven't seen Rafe since I returned."

"Really?" Jason frowned at his half-eaten burger. "That's strange."

Lauren didn't think Rafe's remoteness was strange at all, especially if he'd reverted to the moody man she'd met on her first trip to Cedar Creek.

"Hey, here comes Rafe," Lauren heard Chad say excitedly.

"Well, speaking of the devil," Jason drawled, humor in his voice.

Lauren's heart slammed against her chest, and she forced herself to remain calm when her instincts clamored for her to jump up from her seat and run to greet Rafe. He wasn't here for her, she told herself. He'd come to see Chad.

Following Jason's lead, she stood, her gaze landing on Rafe's truck and the horse trailer he had in tow. He parked his vehicle, and as soon as he stepped out of the cab Chad hurled himself into Rafe's arms.

"Uncle Rafe," Chad said exuberantly, causing smiles and laughter to ripple through the crowd of guests.

They ended the hug, and Rafe grinned at Chad, stealing Lauren's breath with that handsome transformation. "Welcome home, cowboy," he said, tugging on the Stetson on the boy's head. "I brought you a present."

"Yeah?" Chad's eyes rounded in excitement. "What is it?"

"She's right in here." Rafe indicated the trailer. As everyone watched, the pair made their way to the tailgate, which Rafe unlatched and lowered. A moment later, a beautiful chestnut neighed her greeting to Chad and nuzzled his cheek.

"Bronwyn!" Chad glanced from the horse to Rafe, disbelief shining in his eyes. "She's mine?"

"Yep. As long as you promise to take good care of her." Rafe retrieved something from the cab of the truck and presented a shining silver buckle to Chad. "And I thought you might like to wear this. It's the belt buckle I won at my first rodeo when I was about your age."

"Wow!" Chad breathed. "You're the best, Uncle Rafe!"

The complimentary murmurs Lauren heard from the people around her affirmed Chad's declaration.

Rafe's reputation had taken a turn for the better, and the town's hero no longer seemed to resent his status.

Rafe helped Chad secure Bronwyn in an empty paddock, then spent a good fifteen minutes shaking hands and greeting guests, never once looking her way. Lauren watched him from beneath the large shade tree in Kristin's yard as he spoke amicably with everyone and even laughed and smiled. The moody, surly man she'd left behind a month ago seemed to have found a new lease on life, and though Lauren was happy that he'd made peace with himself, she couldn't help but ache for what *they'd* lost.

It seemed like forever before he sought her out, and when he did, she melted inside, because he looked so gorgeous and sexy and very, very confident. One of those tantalizing smiles curved his lips, and he strode purposefully toward her, his gaze holding hers. With every step he took in her direction, her pulse fluttered wildly. The despair she'd experienced a moment ago blossomed into a glimmer of optimism.

He reached her, and paying no mind to the fact that everyone was watching them, he slid his hands into her hair, tilted her face up and kissed her...deeply, passionately, urgently. And because she loved him, she didn't temper her response.

By the time Rafe finished kissing her senseless, the crowd around them was clapping and whistling their approval, and the man in front of her had the most adorable, lopsided grin on his face.

She stared at him, so many doubts clashing with the hope swirling within her. "What was that for?"

His grin deepened, and his gray eyes took on a

mischievous sparkle. "For being such a jerk the last time you were here."

She touched her tongue to her bottom lip, still reeling from his unexpected and very passionate reception. "Well, you certainly have a way with an apology."

"There's a whole lot more where that came from. I've got a lot of groveling to do." Before she could reply to that, he grasped her hand and led her through the throng of people to his truck.

She slid into the passenger seat and waited until he was behind the wheel. "Where are we going?"

He glanced at her, suddenly looking nervous. "I've got something important to show you."

"All right," she said softly, not sure what to expect.

In silence, Rafe drove the truck to the main road and turned toward his ranch. A minute later, he eased the vehicle to the side of the road in front of what used to be a dirt lane leading to his spread. It was now replaced with an asphalt drive. The No Trespassing sign was gone, and white wrought iron gates enclosed the ranch. A matching archway spanned the drive, and an attached paper banner welcomed visitors to...Bright Beginnings.

Stunned, Lauren exited the truck, staring at the astonishing changes Rafe had made in her absence. Part of her conversation with Jason flitted through her mind, making her realize that the town had been in on this surprise of Rafe's.

Warm, gentle hands settled on her shoulders, and the heat of Rafe's body touched her spine. "What do you think?" he asked, uncertainty deepening his voice.

She turned in his embrace, searching his features, afraid to assume anything. "I don't understand. What does all this mean?"

"It means I'm done running from my past, and I'm ready to start my future, with you, here on my ranch." He brushed his fingers along her cheek, his touch reverent. "And if I mean to keep you here, I'd better get used to a steady stream of foster kids visiting us and using our horseback riding facilities."

Her breath caught. He remembered her distant dreams for Bright Beginnings. Now he was offering his ranch as a haven for special foster kids, a place that would offer them happy memories. His unselfish gesture spoke volumes, yet she needed more assurances. "You really want me to stay?"

"Yeah, I do. This past month without you has been more miserable than the past year." He paused as if searching for the right words to persuade her. "I need you in my life, Lauren. I need your smiles and laughter, and I need the way you believe in me when I don't have the courage to believe in myself. I'm hoping you can help me be a better man than my father was."

"Oh, Rafe, you already are." Held in his secure embrace, she could feel his heartbeat, as steady and sure as her own. "You're kind and compassionate, and I'll spend every day reminding you of that."

"And what about your parents?"

"This is my choice, Rafe, not theirs," she said adamantly, knowing her parents would accept her decision. "All I want is to be with the man I love. Everything else will work itself out. I already told you that I can take my foundation anywhere, and this is where my heart is."

He grinned, dazzling her with that gorgeous smile she intended to see as often as possible. "Then I guess there's only one thing left to do."

Anticipation sped up her pulse. "And what's that?"

"Get married. I love you, Lauren." Their gazes locked, the proof of his words shining in his pewter eyes. "And I was thinking maybe we could give Chad a cousin or two...."

"Yes," she whispered around the tears crowding her throat. "Oh, yes!" Wrapping her arms around his neck, she hugged him fiercely, realizing in that moment that all her wishes and dreams had come true.

EPILOGUE

FOUR years later, Lauren's dreams had developed beyond her wildest imaginings, all with the support of her loving husband. Rafe's ranch was the focal point of the weekend camp established for underprivileged children. Bright Beginnings Horseback Adventures had become a project embraced by the entire community. The men in town had assisted Rafe in building a small cabin on the property designed to accommodate four children and two adults. The residents of Cedar Creek donated their time to assist the kids on their weekend visits. Fran's Diner supplied supper for the four children, and others contributed spare time in whatever capacity Lauren needed. Chad, now thirteen, was always present, welcoming the kids and befriending them.

Three weekends out of the month were total, wonderful chaos. The rest of the time Lauren devoted to her husband and three-year-old daughter, Melissa—fondly nicknamed Missy by her cousin. Lauren's life was hectic and busy, but she wouldn't have it any other way. She enjoyed spending time with the children who visited Bright Beginnings, and she loved being Rafe's wife and Missy's mom.

Releasing a contented sigh, Lauren headed out of the office Rafe had built onto the house for her and went in search of her husband and daughter. She'd spent the morning making arrangements with a foster agency in Cody for the arrival of the next group of kids, then had made a quick call to Dr. Kendal's office to confirm a more significant advent.

She had some exciting news to share with her husband.

Crossing the yard toward the paddock where Rafe was helping Missy into a saddle in front of Chad, Lauren smiled as she remembered Rafe's response when he'd learned of her unplanned pregnancy with Missy. Once the initial shock had ebbed, uncertainties and doubts had instantly developed, rendering the father-to-be a nervous wreck. In the eight months he'd had to adjust to the idea of being a dad, they'd managed to work through his fears. As soon as the warm bundle had been placed in his arms and his daughter gazed up at him with wide, unfocused eyes, he'd fallen head over heels in love with her.

The two adored one another, and over the past three years Rafe had proved to be a gentle, compassionate and very patient father.

"Hi, Momma!" Missy greeted her, waving enthusiastically from atop the docile mare. "Chad's taking me for a ride on the big horse!"

Lauren grinned at the pint-size Stetson Missy wore and the leather cowgirl boots with fringe Rafe had insisted on buying her. Chad sat behind her, holding her securely, looking happy and carefree. Missy loved to ride with her cousin, and Chad doted on her.

Stepping into the paddock and leaning against the fence, Lauren waved at the duo as Rafe led them to the open gate. "You two have fun," she called.

"We will," Chad said, then spurred the horse into a trot that had Missy bouncing and giggling with delight.

Rafe made his way to Lauren, his gaze riveted to

Chad and Missy. From beneath the brim of his hat, Lauren saw the worry creasing his brow. For all of Rafe's tenderness, he was fiercely protective of his daughter and still worried over some things.

"Go faster!" Missy squealed, and Chad urged the mare to increase her speed.

Rafe scowled, and just as he started to say something, Lauren pressed her palm over his mouth, muffling the words, "Slow down."

"They're just fine," she admonished gently, moving her hand away. "Chad is very responsible, and not only do you have Missy secured to the saddle, Chad has hold of her, too."

He relented with a grouchy noise that made Lauren smile, and he grinned impishly. His smiles and laughter were no longer a rarity. The women in his life had given him too much joy and happiness to squander it on frowns. She kissed him softly on his lips, just for the heck of it—and because she liked seeing the desire for her flare to life in his gaze. She marveled at the fact that their marriage was more passionate than ever.

Rafe rested his arm around her waist and drew her close, and together they resumed watching Missy. After a quiet moment, she said, "I've confirmed our four arriving guests for Friday."

"Great," he said, his voice low and deep, if not a little preoccupied with his daughter's ride. "Everything is ready for this weekend."

She snuggled closer to him, inhaling his warm, masculine scent. "And I just received confirmation on another arrival for seven months from now."

He cast her a quizzical glance. "Are sure you want to start booking that far in advance?"

"I don't really have a choice on this one," she said with a soft sigh. "Our son or daughter will be arriving whether we're ready or not."

His entire body tensed, and he gaped at her. "You're pregnant?"

"Yeah," she whispered, and waited for his reaction.

She'd expected more worry, more doubts, but the emotion that transformed his expression was pure excitement. Then he twirled her in his arms and laughed, the sound rich and robust and filled with joy. And when she was dizzy and breathless, he kissed her, consuming her with his love.

"You're smooching *again?*" Lauren heard Missy say from somewhere nearby.

"Grown-ups do that," Chad told her importantly, as if he was an authority.

Both adults laughed, breaking the kiss, though Rafe still held her close in his embrace.

Staring at her gorgeous cowboy, Lauren pressed her hand to his cheek. "Have I told you lately that you're my hero?"

He rolled his eyes at her question. "Only every day since we got married."

"Do you believe it?"

The corner of his mouth hitched up in a sexy smile, and he didn't hesitate with his answer. "Yeah, I do."

Sometimes a man needs a little help...

Hiring Ms. Right

*Three single women,
one home-help agency and
three professional bachelors
in need of a...wife?*

Look out for **Leigh Michaels**'s delightful new trilogy:

HUSBAND ON DEMAND
April 2000 (#3600)

BRIDE ON LOAN
May 2000 (#3604)

WIFE ON APPROVAL
June 2000 (#3608)

Available at your favorite retail outlet.

HARLEQUIN®
Makes any time special.™

Visit us at www.romance.net

HRHMR

If you enjoyed what you just read,
then we've got an offer you can't resist!

Take 2 bestselling love stories FREE!

Plus get a FREE surprise gift!

Clip this page and mail it to Harlequin Reader Service®

IN U.S.A.
3010 Walden Ave.
P.O. Box 1867
Buffalo, N.Y. 14240-1867

IN CANADA
P.O. Box 609
Fort Erie, Ontario
L2A 5X3

YES! Please send me 2 free Harlequin Romance® novels and my free surprise gift. Then send me 4 brand-new novels every month, which I will receive months before they're available in stores. In the U.S.A., bill me at the bargain price of $2.90 plus 25¢ delivery per book and applicable sales tax, if any*. In Canada, bill me at the bargain price of $3.34 plus 25¢ delivery per book and applicable taxes**. That's the complete price and a savings of over 10% off the cover prices—what a great deal!! I understand that accepting the 2 free books and gift places me under no obligation ever to buy any books. I can always return a shipment and cancel at any time. Even if I never buy another book from Harlequin, the 2 free books and gift are mine to keep forever. So why not take us up on our invitation. You'll be glad you did!

116 HEN CNEP
316 HEN CNEQ

Name	(PLEASE PRINT)	
Address	Apt.#	
City	State/Prov.	Zip/Postal Code

* Terms and prices subject to change without notice. Sales tax applicable in N.Y.
** Canadian residents will be charged applicable provincial taxes and GST.
   All orders subject to approval. Offer limited to one per household.
   ® are registered trademarks of Harlequin Enterprises Limited.

HROM99   ©1998 Harlequin Enterprises Limited

Mother's Day is Around the Corner...
Give the gift that celebrates Life and Love!

Show Mom you care by presenting her with a one-year subscription to:

HARLEQUIN
WORLD'S BEST
Romances

For only $4.96—
That's 75% off the cover price.

This easy-to-carry, compact magazine delivers 4 exciting romance stories by some of the very best romance authors in the world.

Plus each issue features personal moments with the authors, author biographies, a crossword puzzle and more...

A one-year subscription includes 6 issues full of love, romance and excitement to warm the heart.

To send a gift subscription, write the recipient's name and address on the coupon below, enclose a check for $4.96 and mail it today. In a few weeks, we will send you an acknowledgment letter and a special postcard so you can notify this lucky person that a fabulous gift is on the way!

Yes! I would like to purchase a one-year gift subscription (that's 6 issues) of WORLD'S BEST ROMANCES, for only $4.96. I save over 75% off the cover price of $21.00.   MRGIFT00

This is a special gift for:

Name _____

Address _____ Apt# _____

City _____ State _____ Zip _____

From _____

Address _____ Apt# _____

City _____ State _____ Zip _____

Mail to: HARLEQUIN WORLD'S BEST ROMANCES
P.O. Box 37254, Boone, Iowa, 50037-0254 Offer valid in the U.S. only.

It's hard to resist the lure of the
Australian Outback

One of Harlequin Romance's
best-loved Australian authors

Margaret Way
brings you

Look for

A WIFE AT KIMBARA (#3595)
March 2000

THE BRIDESMAID'S WEDDING (#3607)
June 2000

THE ENGLISH BRIDE (#3619)
September 2000

Available at your favorite retail outlet.

Visit us at www.romance.net   HROUT

Return to the charm of the Regency era with

GEORGETTE
HEYER,

creator of the modern Regency genre.

Enjoy six romantic collector's editions with forewords by some of today's bestselling romance authors,

**Nora Roberts, Mary Jo Putney,
Jo Beverley, Mary Balogh,
Theresa Medeiros and Kasey Michaels.**

Frederica
On sale February 2000
The Nonesuch
On sale March 2000
The Convenient Marriage
On sale April 2000
Cousin Kate
On sale May 2000
The Talisman Ring
On sale June 2000
The Corinthian
On sale July 2000

Available at your favorite retail outlet.

HARLEQUIN®
Makes any time special ™

Visit us at www.romance.net

PHGHGEN

Harlequin Romance®

Women are thin on the ground on Merit Island!

Brothers Jake, Marc and Zach have everything—
except that one special woman.
Can love find a way to win
their lonely, stubborn hearts?

Find out in

RENEE ROSZEL'S
latest miniseries

THE MERITS OF MARRIAGE

HONEYMOON HITCH April 2000 #3599
COMING HOME TO WED May 2000 #3603
with Zach Merit's story to come in 2001

Available at your favorite retail outlet.

HARLEQUIN®
Makes any time special.™

Visit us at www.romance.net

HRMOM

Back by popular demand are

DEBBIE MACOMBER's

Hard Luck, Alaska, is a
town that needs women!
And the O'Halloran brothers
are just the fellows
to fly them in.

Starting in March 2000 this beloved series returns
in special 2-in-1 collector's editions:

MAIL-ORDER MARRIAGES, featuring
Brides for Brothers and *The Marriage Risk*
On sale March 2000

FAMILY MEN, featuring
Daddy's Little Helper and *Because of the Baby*
On sale July 2000

THE LAST TWO BACHELORS, featuring
Falling for Him and *Ending in Marriage*
On sale August 2000

Collect and enjoy each MIDNIGHT SONS story!

Available at your favorite retail outlet.

Visit us at www.romance.net   PHMS

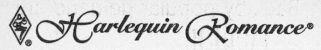

Harlequin Romance®

**On their very special day,
these brides and grooms are determined
the bride should wear white...
which means keeping passion in check!**

WHITE WEDDINGS

True love is worth waiting for...

Enjoy these brand-new stories from
your favorite authors

MATILDA'S WEDDING (HR #3601)
by **Betty Neels**
April 2000

THE FAITHFUL BRIDE
by **Rebecca Winters**
Coming in 2000

Available at your favorite retail outlet, only from

HARLEQUIN®
Makes any time special.™

Visit us at www.romance.net

HRWW2